LETTERS TO ANOTHER

A SHORT STORY COLLECTION

T J BAINZ

CONTENTS

THE LUNCH CROWD

1

THE LUNCH CROWD—or The Lunch Crowd as Kirstee termed them inside her own mind—were like a flock of migratory birds.

That was to say that they flapped about between themselves, day after day after day, they passed from the watering hole—the coffee room—to the boxy park on the corner with their packed lunches—if it was sunny—or to the dainty little lunchroom-slash-cafeteria-thing if there was so much as a spot of rain hanging about in the air.

Kirstee remembered reading something—or had she heard it? —that had said that birds never flew when it rained.

Sounded *a bit* like an urban myth to her, not that natural matters mattered all that much, not from where she sat, on her squeaky desk chair at her radioactive CRT computer monitor, complete with beige, stain-glazed keyboard and sticky mouse.

Kirstee breathed in deeply. Took in the multi-stench of cologne and perfume that floated about the open-plan office. That stench which the flimsy plasterboards between workstations did next to nothing to prevent . . . actually, much closer to *nothing* . . .

She hated this time in the morning. Stuck in that no man's land between arrival and lunch. That period of time which The Lunch Crowd would have termed the Coffee Break. The time when the Lunch Crowd migrated to the coffee room.

But Kirstee didn't drink coffee.

Never had.

Never would.

All her thirty-two years of life she'd avoided it.

Why start now?

That sour, cigarette-butt-like taste just sent her nerves twisting and twirling.

And not in a good way.

As she tapped away at her keyboard, only punctuating the tapping with the odd *click* of a mouse button, she felt a slight churning in her stomach.

That sign she'd learned to recognise as hunger.

Had learned *not* to underestimate to her peril.

She drew in another breath, another of those things that she liked to term 'future sighs' and she reached out and slid open the top drawer in her plasticky, kind of wood-like desk, and pawed through the wreckage there: through the uncoupled, bent-up staples, the seemingly hundreds of chewed and blunted pencils, the broken and—somehow—*dusty* rubber bands.

Nope. No food there.

But what had she expected?

She was always going on at herself, on the bus home at night when she'd press her forehead—ever so gently—up against the window and stare out at the passing landscape, that she had to get into the habit of stocking up her desk.

It seemed like she got like this every day.

Around ten thirty, eleven, she began to tremble with hunger.

And not so much as a biscuit to dull it until lunch.

It made working intolerable.

She had measured her productivity, discovered that it declined by no less than twelve point seven percent at this time of day . . . she guessed that she was somewhat lucky her boss hadn't yet cottoned onto this.

No, she needed to make changes, and make them fast.

Her stomach gave another lurch.

This time she was ready for it.

She squeezed her stomach in on itself, hoping to stop the sounds dead.

No such luck.

Her stomach grumbled long and it grumbled loud.

She noticed Stephen—the guy who shared her workstation cubicle—give her a quick glance over his shoulder, adjust his metal-framed glasses, give her the hint of a smile and then turn his attention back to his own computer monitor.

Stephen wasn't part of The Lunch Crowd, and Kirstee was glad.

Though she never would've said so much aloud.

She could barely bring herself to imagine how it might be, how The Lunch Crowd might swoop on by to pick Stephen up, sweep him along in their flock to wherever their migratory pattern dictated they go at that specific time of day.

Oh, Kirstee had no *sexual* feelings for Stephen.

For one, Stephen was married with a wife and kids, and though some women might've seen that as a challenge—no doubt as a sort of 'turn on'—the truth was that Kirstee had never really *had* sexual feelings.

Not about anyone.

Or any*thing*.

She was just content with what she had.

With her life, her job, her *routine*.

Day in, day out.

If only she could—somehow—dispense with The Lunch Crowd, she knew that her life would be immeasurably better.

But it didn't seem like there were any fairies bobbing about—no genies in lamps either—ready and willing to grant a girl's innermost wish . . .

Kirstee sniffed. Glanced at the clock. This *was* her coffee break.

Right now. She was *entitled* to take the fifteen minutes. To go and have a little time off. Some time to herself. But she never liked to leave her desk till lunch. Didn't want to run the risk of running into one of *them*.

Today, though . . . well, that was the rub of it . . . today was . . . it was *different*.

Today felt like one of those watershed days, one of those days where things just sort of got changed up—the old gave way to the new . . .

She quietly resolved that no more would she suffer here, at her desk alone, without anything at all to eat.

No, there was a vending machine.

Not far from here.

Half a minute—a *whole* minute at most.

She would just have to take the first step.

And so, pulling her fuzzy, turquoise jumper down to cover the waistband of her sensible, black, ankle-high skirt, she hauled herself onto her feet, adjusted her large, plastic-framed glasses, pushed them back a little on her nose so they wouldn't slip into the sweatier lower half, and she marched onwards.

On her quest.

THE VENDING MACHINE gave very few options.

Very few options for Kirstee, in any case.

The problem as she saw it—well, as she guessed she'd *always* seen it—was that she seemed to be allergic to planet Earth.

Hay fever, lactose intolerance, gluten . . . *Jesus*, if she got started into thinking about *gluten* then she might well end up standing here all day . . . and she was *quite certain* her boss would have a few things to say about *that*.

She stared through the slick glass of the vending machine, took in the options again, the products all slipped into their little metal coils, the machine blinking its red-neon lettering at her, just inviting her to drop a coin in and see what happened.

Chocolate.

Packets of crisps.

A couple of 'fruit-flavoured' beverages.

. . . Really nothing at all for Kirstee.

Nothing that *appealed* to her in any case.

And so, arching her shoulders back, digging deep, right to the pits of her lungs, she sighed out an almighty sigh, a sigh which—in her mind's eye—caused a tornado to spin out of her, and to wreak havoc across the entire office . . . tossing up cubicles, computer monitors, desk chairs alike . . .

When she'd recovered from said sigh, she noticed the presence of someone standing near at her shoulder. She turned to look and saw that it was Sara, from Marketing.

Today Sara wore a silk, violet blouse which met in a V-shape at her bust, just revealing a little cleavage on its way. She wore it over a pair of stone-washed blue jeans which Kirstee did not think *quite* adequate for the workplace.

But what did *she* know, she wasn't Sara's boss.

In fact, Kirstee had as little to do with marketing as she could possibly manage.

"Hey," Sara said, the smile not only on her lips but in her voice too.

Kirstee, who often admitted to herself that she'd never really *got* smiling, did her best to return the sentiment. But, on reflection, she was pretty sure it turned out way more like a smirk than a smile.

Then again, what did she really care.

Sara was one of them.

One of the Lunch Crowd.

"Good Morning," Kirstee finally got out.

Sara glanced to Kirstee, then looked to the vending machine, she pouted a little. "Not going to get anything, then?"

Kirstee shrugged. "There doesn't seem to be much *choice*."

"In that case, do you mind if I . . . ?" and then she made a slight gesture with her hands which Kirstee guessed was supposed to signify her slipping past her, going to the machine herself.

Kirstee relented—allowed Sara past.

For some reason, and even reflecting on it later, Kirstee couldn't quite tell *why* she hung back from the vending machine, deciding *not* to return directly to her desk, as was usual protocol whenever she ran into a member of the Lunch Crowd . . . or, to be a little more honest about it, anyone at all who did their best to ensnare her in conversation.

Maybe it was because—that particular day—she was especially hungry, and hadn't *quite* given up on perhaps getting something out of the vending machine.

Sara slotted a few coins through the slit.

Kirstee listened to the *ka-thunk* as they passed through the mechanism and then the metal *splash* as they landed in the unseen repository within.

It was like she was hypnotised—*yes*, something like that.

Kirstee found herself rooted to the spot.

As Sara went about jabbing her choice into the accompanying keypad of the vending machine, she spoke out of the corner of her mouth, as if Kirstee hanging back at her shoulder, skulking about, was just the most natural thing in the world.

"So," Sara said, "Got any plans for lunch today?"

Kirstee was caught totally off guard by the question. It was something that she could never have imagined in a thousand years —in a thousand *nightmares*. And yet, here it was, very much being asked, and so directly.

Kirstee blinked a few times, blew out an inaudible half sigh wondering what excuse she might give . . . but, after a few seconds' thought, she came up with nothing . . . nothing at all, she felt like she had no imagination to come up with a single reason.

The thing that Sara chose from the machine turned out to be a chocolate bar wrapped in a lurid, shiny purple wrapper. It dropped with a *thunk* at the base of the machine. Sara pushed her hand through the flap which gave a sharp *squeal* of its hinges. On her way back up, she slipped Kirstee a sidelong glance. "Because," Sara said, "If you've got no plans then I was wondering if you'd like to do something with us—if you'd like to come to lunch with us?"

So, there it was.

An *invitation*.

And for Kirstee, exclusively.

Though she knew it was ridiculous to think so, she found herself momentarily transported back to school, to the *bullies* at school—those unkind girls who would invite her to their houses, to their parties, and then go away giggling behind their hands as if they thought that Kirstee hadn't cottoned on to their attempted barbs . . . Kirstee had *never* understood how girls could fall for things like that, how there might actually exist girls so socially rejected—let's *face* it, like *her*—who would be so desperate as to venture on out to those false, never-would-be invitations with soul-destroying hope . . .

And yet, this was the *workplace*.

There would be *punishments—consequences—*for those who got involved in such playground antics.

No, she was overreacting, she was sure of it.

Still, she wanted to know more before she reached her decision.

And so she looked to Sara—looked to those pale-green eyes of hers, and those *fragile* features of hers—and she said, "Why me?"

"Excuse me?" Sara said, pouting a little as she tore the wrapper of the chocolate bar.

"Why are you asking *me?*"

Sara's lips parted a little as if she was on the cusp of giving an explanation. Then she checked herself. Said nothing at all for the time being. She turned her attention back down to the chocolate bar in her hands and her continuing wrestle with the wrapper, and then finally got out, "Just seen you about here, I mean, sort of, well . . . *alone,* and thought you might want to hang around with us at lunchtime. Get to know other people about the office, that sort of thing."

Kirstee scoffed inwardly at the childish phrasing of 'hanging around' with them, this really was like one of those schoolyard scenes of hers revisited.

And yet . . . and yet there *was* a part of her which was curious.

Intensely curious.

Curious to know what it really might be like.

To run with the Lunch Crowd.

Sara tore the wrapper clean off her chocolate bar, snapped off one of the quadrants of chocolate and then extended it towards Kirstee—a peace-offering of sorts.

Kirstee held up her hand. Summoned a smile. "No, thank you," she said. "I'm allergic."

Sara's lips parted in that way of hers again, sort of halfway between confusion and understanding.

Kirstee sucked in a good lungful of air, looked about the office, glanced about the various cubicles all nested about there, she looked back to her own desk, to her computer, and to Stephen still sat in his own chair, tapping away at his keyboard.

Then she turned back to Sara.

Took her in.

Felt all-new feelings rippling through her.

She hardly knew what she was saying when she said, "All right, that'd be lovely."

Sara gave her a faint smile and then, chomping on her chocolate, trotted back off to her own desk in the Marketing Department.

S TRANGELY, Kirstee noted a positive five-percent increase in her productivity by the time the clock at the corner of her computer screen ticked onto twelve thirty.

Lunchtime.

Instinctively, she glanced about her as if expecting to find the Lunch Crowd had sprung up about her while she'd been engrossed in her work.

They hadn't of course.

That would have just been silly.

Kirstee felt a slight tingle in her back. Nerves, perhaps? She could feel a slight tremble taking her over. All those old hang-ups seemed to return to her for a moment . . . all the *bad* girls from school, the ones who'd made her feel like an idiot.

The ones she'd sworn never to think about again for as long as she lived.

. . . And now she'd gone and failed at doing so.

She toyed with the idea of staying her ground, of keeping her head below the line of sight of her cubicle and hoping the Lunch Crowd didn't notice her, but she discarded that idea, deciding that now she'd made the choice, it was something which she should stick with.

And so she clambered up to her feet, glancing briefly to Stephen—still sat at his desk behind her, chomping on a sandwich, and catching the crumbs of it in a translucent, plastic container.

She made it over to the doorway where she knew the Lunch Crowd always met and, sure enough, found them all waiting there.

Chattering away, quite happily.

All dozen or so of them.

She couldn't quite comprehend the sight before her, mostly

because she'd witnessed it daily since . . . well, pretty much ever since she started off at the company, started working here, a good ten years ago now.

And now she was *one* of them.

Sara spotted her before she spotted Sara, and she swaggered on up to her, that silky violet blouse of hers shimmering in the fluorescent light of the office. Sara was smiling thickly and, apparently, without irony.

Kirstee did her best to smile back.

"Great of you to join us," Sara said.

"Nice to be invited," Kirstee replied.

Sara kept up her smile and Kirstee detected no impending failure in it, no sign that she was faking it 'to be nice', that aspect she'd always feared about *other people*.

But, then again, people could be devious.

"Did you bring lunch?" Sara said.

Kirstee shook her head. "No, I never do—I like to go to the sandwich shop on the corner of the street . . . it's the best place to get something fast to eat at lunchtime."

"*Delorey's?*" Sara said.

Kirstee felt her chest tighten just a little. It was strange. She wasn't really sure *why* she felt a little uncomfortable about this prospect. After all she did realise that there were other people in the world—and that those other people inhabited the same parts that she did.

"That's right," Kirstee finally replied.

Sara cocked her head to one side. And her smile widened even further, if anything. "I love going there—that's where we were thinking of going today, then going down into the park, to sit there and eat."

Kirstee almost had the urge to butt in, to tell Sara that she knew all about the Lunch Crowd's games. She had been a watcher, after all. Someone had to be.

Now would she really be one of them?

Was this what she *really* wanted?

It was odd how the Lunch Crowd moved. If there was a leader, someone who was showing them the direction, making the plans, then Kirstee couldn't have said exactly who it was. The whole mass —the dozen or so people—all still chattering away happily: men in suits and ties, some wearing jackets, others not, women in their blouses, clutching handbags, clacking along in heels, sort of seemed to move off as one great big congealed mass, gradually oozing its way out through the office, overspilling into the street, and then making some sort of relentless progress towards the park.

Being up close was a different prospect.

Kirstee saw that now.

When she'd been an observer she had been afraid—been afraid to get too close to them and to make any sort of in-detail observation.

She had never studied how they'd moved, at least.

And it was odd to think that now—now that she was moving among them . . . if she couldn't say that she was *part* of them . . . it all seemed so natural, almost as if she no longer had to think for herself any longer.

She paced alongside Sara who had brought another girl with her, a girl called Jessica, as she'd introduced her to Kirstee. The two of them continued to chatter away amongst themselves and Kirstee was glad—glad that she wouldn't have to make conversation, answer, no doubt, inane questions about her life.

About things which *other people* had no business in prying into.

When they reached the sandwich shop, they sort of flooded the place out.

All of them filing along—in line—to get their sandwiches.

That was one thing that Kirstee *certainly* found different.

Back on her own she had *always* arrived here, to *Delorey's*, ahead of the Lunch Crowd.

That was one of the benefits of moving about the place alone.

The mobility of it . . . being nimble on your feet.

And now she formed part of the snaking queue which slithered through the sandwich shop, the attendant taking their orders—one by one—she realised how much time they devoted to their single mass, to, for one reason or another, their staying together.

When her turn arrived, Kirstee ordered her usual.

The one sandwich that met *all* her requirements.

Gluten-free bread.

Ham in the middle.

Nothing else.

She even got a smile off the shopkeeper there, the first time *that* had ever happened.

She wondered if he recognised her, or if—more to the point—he *didn't* recognise her . . . if only now, now that she was part of this singular organism dubbed the Lunch Crowd, he actually acknowledged her existence.

Why, she'd been coming in here at least once a week for the entire time she'd worked at the company . . . he *should* have remembered her name, surely.

He couldn't have had more than a thousand customers a week at any rate—and much fewer of those would've been *repeat* customers, like her.

Then again, she guessed she didn't really know much about it at all.

She didn't really know *much* about the real world at all.

Sandwich in hand, and remaining in the vicinity of the Lunch Crowd, Kirstee followed them across the street and to the park.

She eyed—not a little wistfully—the bench a long way back, half-hidden in overgrown bushes, where she would normally sit to eat her sandwich.

She wondered if anyone ever saw her there.

If they ever *noticed* her sitting there.

Watching everyone.

4

KIRSTEE FOLLOWED Sara and Jessica over to a patch of grass, at which point Sara rocked her large handbag back to her elbow and pried through it, finally removing a rug which she had folded up inside. Between the two of them, Jessica and Sara laid the rug down on the grass, flattening it out with their hands. And just then—right when Kirstee had half convinced herself that Jessica and Sara had forgotten that she was even there —they both turned to her and invited her to sit.

Kirstee hesitated a moment then accepted their offer.

Kirstee *never* sat on the grass . . . not even with a rug beneath her.

Now that she did, she found it strangely springy and—dare she say it—a fairly *pleasant* experience. Even though she was certain she could feel the beginnings of a rash already emerging.

As they munched through their sandwiches, Sara turned her attention to Kirstee. "So," she said, "How come we never see you out and about much?"

Kirstee turned her words over in her mind, but, at the same time, couldn't help repeating them out loud. ". . . 'Out and about'?"

"Yeah," Sara said, with a smile, mouth full of chewed-up sandwich. "Don't you think it's funny how we all work in the same place and we hardly ever see one another—hardly ever realise we even work at the same company."

But Kirstee *had* seen Sara before . . . Jessica too . . . and though she hadn't been able to assign them their appropriate names— obviously—Kirstee did feel a slight sting that she had become so *invisible* to them, so unsubstantial that they could merely write her off as not even existing at all.

But this was the life she'd chosen.

What she'd chosen to do when she'd snubbed joining the Lunch Crowd when, surely, she'd had the chance to do so many years ago.

She'd *decided* to keep to herself.

Maintain her private profile.

Hadn't she?

And it was for this reason that Kirstee settled on a simple, "Yes," in answer to Sara's question, and then turned to look out over the greenery of the park.

Sara went on to ask all the usual questions—how long Kirstee had worked for the company—'ten years, give or take, her whole working life', what she did exactly—'accounting', and what she liked to do for fun at the weekends—'read books, watch films and TV'... and then the conversation took a more bizarre turn.

"Do you like walking at all?" Sara said.

"What?" Kirstee replied.

"Walking—like *hill* walking?"

"I, uh"—Kirstee slipped Jessica a glance, saw that she was looking just about as eager as Sara was—"I can't say that I've ever tried it... but, I uh..."

Jessica took this as her cue to break in. "We've been wanting to put together a club," she said. "Our own *hill* walking club."

"Oh?" Kirstee said, a little beleaguered at all of this stuff coming at her.

"Yeah," Sara said, taking up Jessica's slack, and then, looking about herself, she lowered her tone, and continued, "We've been wondering if you'd be interested in joining."

" 'In joining' ?" Kirstee repeated.

Jessica cupped her hands about her mouth, mimicking a megaphone, and then said, loudly, "Looks like we've got an echo, *echo, echo, echo* ... here, *here, here, here* ..."

Sara sniffed a laugh.

Kirstee managed to raise a dry chuckle though she didn't find the joke all that funny.

Jessica and Sara exchanged glances and there was something—some *odd* interaction between the two of them that Kirstee just couldn't place . . . but she could say for certain that it *was* there.

Like a twinkle passing between their eyes.

But as soon as she'd noticed, it seemed to vanish right away.

"Wanna know what we're thinking of calling it?" Sara said.

"Okay?" Kirstee said, with a slight shrug.

Sara and Jessica again traded one of those conspiratorial glances, then Sara said, *"Lezzers in Leathers."*

Funnily enough, thinking back on the occasion later that evening, Kirstee wasn't sure why she said, " *'In Leathers'* ?" as if that was the most important part of the statement Sara had just made.

Sara gave her a squint-eyed grin then replied, "Because of the walking boots," she said.

"Oh," Kirstee said, and then, thinking that she sounded a little dizzy, "the walking boots."

"Small at first—obviously," Sara continued, "but it'll grow, just start out with a few, and that's all it takes really, isn't it?"

Kirstee watched on, paralysed, as Sara laid her hand down onto the back of Jessica's. She watched on as they exchanged what, and she was almost certain of it, was a *loving* glance.

She really had no idea how she'd ended up here.

How having chosen to go with the Lunch Crowd had brought her here.

To *this* venture.

Already, she glanced about, scoping out possibilities to get off the scene. To try and avoid that sure-fire awkwardness that would now follow as she tried to explain her way out of the situation.

Going with the Lunch Crowd—accepting Sara's offer—it'd been a big mistake, she saw that now, and she chided herself for not having seen it before.

It was all about retrospect really, wasn't it?

Retrospect and *bad* choices that couldn't be changed once they'd been made.

Only now, when she glanced back at Sara, back at Jessica, did she see their parted-lipped expressions, maybe the beginnings of some layer of shock.

"Oh," Sara said, "I didn't think to ask, do you have a partner?"

Kirstee blinked a few times. Realised that she still held half her sandwich in her hand. She examined the bite marks she'd left there. The ham in her mouth now tasted overly salty. And a cold sensation drifted through her blood.

She fixed her stare onto Sara. "No," she said, "no I don't."

Sara parted her lips wider. "Ah, that's not a problem, though"—she shifted a sidelong glance at Jessica as if they were operating some telepathic connection—"I mean, that's the whole idea of *Lezzers In Leathers*, to bring people together."

Kirstee first felt the numbness at the very tips of her toes, rippling its way down to her bones ever so gradually. And then in her blood. Creeping up her legs. Into her hips. Her stomach. Her chest—her *heart*—and then, all of a sudden, she felt very distant, almost like she might be watching this scene play out from some-where faraway, though she knew that she still sat there, with the pair of ladies.

With the rest of the Lunch Crowd surrounding her.

It was Sara's voice that finally brought her around.

Saying her name over and over.

"...Stee... Kirstee... Kirstee..."

And, just like that, it was as if Kirstee had shifted out of a profound sleep, like she'd simply dozed off here, on the grass, with the sun on her back, a slight breeze blowing against her cheeks. Now, though, she knew that decisions needed to be made—statements needed laying down—clarifications had to be put out into the open.

"I, uh," Kirstee began, fixing her attention on her sandwich rather than either Sara or Jessica, "I'm *not* . . . ah, one of . . ."

But she had no need to finish her sentence because she heard the *gasp* near enough splitting the air.

When she dared look up, she saw that Sara was wide-eyed —*again*—open-mouthed, and that she held those dainty fingers of hers to her disbelieving lips.

"I . . . I . . ." Sara started, but seemed unable to finish.

"It's okay," Kirstee said, getting up, half-finished sandwich still just about held between her fingers. She gave her skirt a slight brush to clear it of any grass that might've stuck there—and to iron out the firm crease in the front. "I understand," she added.

As Kirstee walked away from Sara and Jessica, making her way across the soft lawn of the park, she couldn't help but allow herself the slither of a smile—just that tiny little flicker of knowledge that *she* had found herself in a situation such as that one. Oh, she wasn't so blinded by her loneliness—to how she *presented* herself—to think that it was a great, big shock . . . because, if she was really truthful towards herself, if she *really* dug deep and told the truth, she had to admit that she was surprised that nobody had approached her earlier, some organising committee, perhaps not *Lezzers In Leathers*, but something else of its ilk . . .

But they didn't know *her* secret.

That she was alone.

Living her life.

To her own tune.

And she supposed that—one day—she might *thank* the Lunch Crowd for having allowed her to gain that insight . . . or she might just rock onwards with her own routine, and choose to keep her nose out of other people's business, just as she'd hope they'd keep *their* noses out of *hers*.

THE DIVISIVE CHORUS

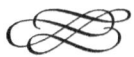

1

THIS MORNING, when Jennifer got up, she felt like her head had been screwed on all wrong. The pressure pushing down on her cranium. The smell of vomit in her nostrils. The slightly *too-clean* taste on her tongue—the one that told her that she'd maybe spent an hour or so with her electric toothbrush buzzing over her gums the night before. And then there was the way the light just beamed on in through her too-thin curtains, bringing sunlight to the backs of her eyelids in the form of bright red rays.

Things would only get worse from here on out.

Of course they would.

How else did she expect it to go?

She screwed up her eyes and peered about the room—to the rolled-up laundry, at least three quarters of it soiled by either urine or sweat, or a combination of the both, that rendered it unusable.

She was looking for that slick, smooth and grey-white container. The one that brought her the happiness, and the one that left her feeling lovesick afterwards.

Like now.

Just like she felt now.

And to be lovesick at forty-nine, why it sent her to despair.

Surely it was *too late* for love now.

Or so she had hoped.

Finally she spotted the container: really a plastic flask of sorts, one of those rectangular bottles with the screw cap designed to keep toddlers from opening it.

And people like *her*.

But, in reality, she knew its secret.

Knew all she had to do was grasp the plastic bottle tightly, push the screw cap down and . . . *twist!*

She shucked her duvet, hearing it slip down onto the floor with that series of tumbling feathers, and whatever else it was they put in duvets.

She wore a nightgown.

That was a minor miracle, all things considered.

It was the light grey one—the one that she'd always imagined was *really* a pale shade of blue, but which people . . . oh, who was she kidding? . . . *lovers* were always telling her was *grey*.

What did *people* really know, anyway?

On her knees, Jennifer scrabbled along the bedroom floor, feeling the scrub of the thick carpet—which always felt much rougher against her skin than she remembered—as she ventured along in search of the plastic, white bottle.

And its sweet label with its baby-blue lettering splashed all over.

Not a trace of *red* anywhere to see.

Finally, she reached it—she reached *out* for it. Took a hold of the bottle in her fist. Brought the bottle up to inspect it a little more closely. And yet, at the same time, treated it with the utmost caution, as if it might have the power to poke her eye out, or something like that.

For a long while—maybe a minute, it might've been more—she simply savoured the moment. This moment where she held the plastic bottle in her hand. Thought she could just about hear the liquid sloshing about inside. Praying for her to toss it back down her throat so that it might leave her with that foaming sensation in her chest. So that it might send those fizzles through her blood and humming direct to her heart.

So that she might sleep a little longer in this *wide-awake* world.

She breathed in, listening to how loud her inhales were in this empty house of hers.

This *detached* house of hers.

A house which could quite easily fit another four—if not more —souls into it.

... But that would've been impossible.

They—whoever *they* were—would ask far too many questions.

And they'd be questions she wouldn't be able to answer.

Perhaps that was why she feared them.

No, it was better like this.

Just her and the house, and her sweet, white plastic bottle here.

And her *elixir* all snug within.

Just as she pushed down on the cap of the bottle, felt the compression work open the safety catch, she heard the birds starting up outside.

The chirruping and twittering.

That old—*same*—divisive chorus.

P EOPLE HAD BEEN SAYING RUBBISH about it for months now, and, to be quite blunt, Jennifer was just well and truly sick of it, who wouldn't be?

Oh, it wasn't that she had *heard* them, because she hadn't.

She *hadn't* heard what it was that her neighbours were saying but that didn't mean that she couldn't *predict* just exactly the words which came out of their mouths: at breakfast, lunch and dinner . . . *criticising* her.

Yes, she had to put up with a *great deal* all things considered.

And that wasn't even the worst of it, either.

Why, she had to put up with it, too, inside of her head.

She had no one else to talk to, after all.

Just me, myself and I . . . all here and alone in this great, big house.

But she drove people away. The people who would steal from her.

Who would make her *change*.

That wouldn't do . . . not at all . . . because she needed her flask of *white stuff* else the world would come to an end, else she wouldn't be able to *function* any longer—whatever *functioning* really meant to her any more.

It must've been around midmorning. At least Jennifer could feel the warming glow in her stomach beginning to fade. And that dizzy, too-slick sharpness of the world coming back into focus about her. That was when she heard the doorbell.

Her heart twitched.

And her blood ran cold.

She couldn't bear it.

Not again.

But she would have to go on . . . yes, that was the cut and thrust of the thing—she would *have* to go on.

As she felt her mind gently stitching itself back together, she noticed the white plastic bottle beside her. It was uncapped, of course, and it was lying on its side. But it had already reached the point where there simply wasn't enough liquid left inside of it for anything to come pouring out through the neck of the bottle.

She was glad, and swept up the bottle as she staggered to her feet, her bare soles slipping on the landing carpet as she brought the front hall into view down below.

Right at the base of the staircase.

Not too far away now.

She held the bottle to her breast, considered her options.

Through the frosted glass which surrounded the front door she could make out shadows—*forms* of people on the other side. The *people* who had rung the bell. Who wanted *her* to come to the door, to bring it open, and to *interface* with her—or so it seemed was the case by her intuition.

Her options appeared very limited all of a sudden, and the brass latch on the back of the door caught a ray of sunshine and a shimmering, seemingly multi-coloured light, passed right over its surface.

She clasped tight to the oak banister—the one she had spent most of the last week polishing—and she clung for dear life as she helped herself down the steps.

One by one . . . one by one . . . just taking them *one by one.*

When she reached the bottom, the smooth, wooden slatted floors which made up the front hall, she felt a little anxious. Could see one of those people pressing their face to the frosted glass. No doubt holding their hand up just at their eyebrows so they might better see.

She hesitated another moment and then, mind made up, clung

on tight to her white plastic bottle and reached for the brass latch .
. . but not before she'd brought the golden chain out—rattling
along the way—and slid it into its housing so the door would not
open more than the width of a foot.

One had to be careful.

Yes, that saying was *true*.

And so, taking extreme care, she extended her crooked fingers
in the direction of the latch, felt its steady weight beneath her
touch and, taking just as much care as she had with everything
else, she brought the front door open.

And found herself staring into the faces of a pair of gentlemen.

Right here.

On her doorstep.

3

J ENNIFER READ THEIR FACES—she'd *always* been good at
reading faces.

And *clothes* too, she'd had a knack for reading people's
clothes.

Suits, that was what they wore.

Those light brown, pretty much *beige* suits.

And *light blue* shirts underneath.

Several shades lighter than her nightdress, though, or so other
people would have told her.

Neither of them wore ties. And they had creases pressed into
their trousers.

One of them was blond, shaved of head, and young-*looking*.

He stood a few paces at his partner's heels, and had a clipboard
dangling from his hands, dangling down at his thigh.

His partner was older. Had black hair with wispy grey tufts
spotted about it. What her mother might've termed *salt-and-pepper*
hair, though Jennifer had always *hated* that phrase. It'd always got
her thinking about hair, and dandruff—all that dried-up, flaky skin
—and it would only serve to turn her stomach, to send a kind of
nausea plummeting to the base of her gut . . . so she didn't think
about it now.

Yes, the *older* partner was perhaps a couple of years younger
than she was, though if she didn't mind saying so, even if it *was*
only inside of her mind, *she* had done a much better job of
preserving her figure—a better job than *he* appeared to have done,
in any case, judging by the podgy beer belly which jiggled out over
the waistband of his trousers.

His complexion was darker than his younger companion's too,

in that olive-skinned way, and Jennifer wondered if maybe the older of the two had a bit of Mediterranean blood about him . . . she had *had* a Mediterranean lover in the past few months—or was it *years?*

When the older of the two spoke to her, his voice was hard, direct. Straight to the point. Just how Jennifer *liked* her men, actually, thinking about it. "Ms Douglas," he began.

"*Mrs,*" she corrected him.

"Yes," the man said, shifting a glance back over his shoulder, to his companion there, still holding the clipboard down at his thigh in a way that made Jennifer feel greatly uneasy.

He looked back to her. "We're from the 'letricity company—jus' come by to run some tests, and tha'."

Something about the man Jennifer found to her extreme distaste.

Was it his tone? That *glottal stop* of his?

How he *cut* his t's right off as if they hadn't existed in the first place?

. . . Perhaps, but there was something else *too.*

Jennifer had always prided herself on her ability to see past such surface details as pronunciation, *diction,* that sort of thing. And she relished her gift for seeing into people's souls—for seeing into the *heart* of a person.

She looked past the man, out to the road outside.

He had a *van* though her eyes were still a little bleary and she couldn't make out the lettering on its side . . . if there was even any lettering at all—wasn't that why they called them white-van men?

She turned back to him. "Do you, uh, happen to have any identification?"

"'Dentification?" he said, with a slight squint, and then a flicker of a smile, as if he'd just remembered. He pawed into the inside pocket of his suit jacket, fished about a while, then produced a laminated piece of plastic which he handed to her.

She took it from him.

It showed the man's mug shot. Unsmiling. His complexion seeming even more *olive*-toned. She could just about see the collar of a dark-blue overall and the neck of a white undershirt. He was looking up in an odd way, as if he was looking up and out past her.

Seeing right *through* her.

She couldn't read any of the words. They just marched about like a hundred unherdable black-and-blue ants. The shiny emblem which she supposed marked authenticity was just as unwieldy— just as incomprehensible to her.

She turned her attention back to the man, only now realising that he'd been speaking while she'd been taking in his identification.

". . . And got the orders right here," he said, nodding to his younger companion who took this as his cue to step forwards with the clipboard held to his chest, concealing the information written out there, clipped to it.

Jennifer shifted her glance from one man to the next. She knew this was suspicious. Knew all about *these* sorts of scams. She read about them in the news when her vision wasn't too bleary, when she hadn't glugged down a little too much of her 'special brew'.

Little old ladies, hustled on their doorsteps by official-looking people who they'd let in, give them a cup of tea, and all the while they'd be casing the whole place, nicking all the silver, the cash stuffed into the mattress and whatever else they could possibly get their filthy paws on. And Jennifer would *not* be like those little old ladies.

She was only forty-*nine* for goodness' sake!

The man was continuing to speak, but his words had long ago pittered out into being animal sounds. She experienced this often.

With the TV, usually. She'd sit herself down. Have a drink. And then everything would just be waves . . . she'd catch little fragments of conversations. The odd word here and there. But in the end she would never be able to keep up. It was like trying to run a marathon while having her feet imbedded in blocks of concrete.

She felt *sluggish* . . . and she was glad now that she had opened the door with the chain engaged, so that these men *would not* force themselves through the crack and into her home.

She felt for her plastic bottle. Allowed her fingers to press a little harder into it.

There was just enough left inside.

Just enough to get her through the rest of the day.

She didn't have to think about tomorrow.

Not *quite* yet . . . and a good thing too considering that it brought her out in a cold sweat.

The man was squinting at her now. His forehead furrowed. He was asking her something. Gesturing at her. At her *chest* . . . at her *bottle* . . . well, he wouldn't have it, of course he wouldn't, he would have to *slay* her first!

She took her chance when he poked his hand through the gap in the door.

Brought the door shut on his fingers.

Listened to his animal *yelp!* as the skin and nerves got trapped.

Gritted her teeth as she prepared to slam it again.

The man only just retrieved his fingers in time.

Just before she did bring the door shut for a final time.

Listened to the slam echo about her home.

The echoes bouncing back at her.

Those sound waves almost seeming to nuzzle and massage her.

And then, as she listened to the grunting—the *shouting*—on the other side of her door, she glanced down to see the man's identification that she still held it tight in her hand.

Had that been what he'd wanted?

Had he just wanted his plastic card back?

To be sure, she crouched down and jabbed the plastic card through the letterbox, listened to it land with a few plasticky clatters on the doorstep outside, and then she shipped on off, into the kitchen, *away* from the front door.

4

NOTHER SIP from the bottle and she felt herself steaming through the world again. Felt herself slipping back into something approaching normality. The liquid slowed her down. Seemed to fix up all her holes—all those holes that'd been torn into her throughout the years, and which she knew would never be mended completely.

Not if she went on living for a thousand more years.

So she had to make adjustments, had to make little *improvisations*.

That was the only way she would be permitted to keep living.

To keep living inside of her own head.

As she propped herself up against the side of the marble kitchen counter, she looked out into the road, to the passing traffic, and to where the men's van had once been.

She had seen them off well.

Had shown them that *This Bitch Bites!*

They would not be back in a hurry.

And the rest of the afternoon passed in a flurry of darkness and light, and the softness of pillows, and finally the security and comfort of her own bed.

5

BEFORE SHE KNEW IT, Jennifer was waking to the night— her least favourite of times, the time when it seemed just like all the evil in the world was *winning*, like she'd just about gone and got herself surrounded, pinned down in her house here.

And like she was being inspected, being poked here, and *there*, searched for any sign of weakness at all so that at just the right moment she would be pounced upon.

The chills only struck her when she stood at her en suite sink, the cold and hot taps both running, and held the white plastic bottle upside down, waiting for so much as a single drip.

But there would be no drip.

She had a faint recollection that, early in the afternoon, in the kitchen, after those . . . those *men*—they *had* been men, hadn't they? . . . had come on by, where she had stood over the kitchen sink, taps running as she ran these taps in the en suite now, and how she'd filled up the bottle all the way, till the water had just reached the very cusp of the neck and she'd seen that milky white liquid inside, all diluted with the water, and how she'd knocked the bottle back and drunk it all down in a series of gulps.

She could still feel the chill as water had streaked down her cheeks in rivulets.

Those lost scraps of the liquid.

And how she'd later got hold of a napkin, dried her face with it, and then sucked at the cloth, doing her best not to think about the roughness of the fabric against her tongue.

And doing quite a bad job of it, considering.

No, right here and now, standing in the en suite, plastic bottle upturned, she knew that she was finished, that she would have no more of her precious liquid.

Not unless she strove out into the Big Bad World.
Did something that could bring them in.
Like a wolf pack.
Surrounding her on all sides.
. . . But didn't she feel surrounded, like, right now?

6

THE SCALE OF THE TASK only struck her while she sat in the garage, in her car, in the rose-red estate which hadn't yet notched up three hundred miles.

Nearly new.

That was what it was.

Almost undriven.

But, at the same time, *not*.

She had the engine running. That hadn't been a difficult task. Just slipping the key fob into this or that hole, then pressing the button that said 'Turn On'.

Made for idiots, really.

The garage doors. There had to be a way to get them open.

Maybe it was a wave of inspiration that struck her, or maybe it was just some voice from the back of her brain that she'd long thought dead, but which had returned to defy her at the very last. But whatever it was, she found herself reaching for the glove compartment undoing the catch, and the spring opening with a potent *wong!*

She pawed about inside for the remote, dug it out, and then squeezed the large red button.

This, also, she found was made for idiots.

The garage door rolled back before her, and the night sky, moon and all, opened out before the bonnet of the car, as if enticing her into her next move.

And she would not now resist.

7

THE INSIDE of the pharmacy was lit with too-bright fluorescent white lights. It had those large windows which occupied the entire side of the building. Everything smelled of disinfectant and that medicinal *sour* note. Really, Jennifer didn't know if she would've been able to bear it, if it hadn't been for the mission she had already embarked on.

One which was, no joke, a matter of life and death.

A teenage girl . . . or maybe she was older, *yes* she *must've* been older, a pharmacist, after all, required a degree, all of that training, all that other stuff that she really didn't . . .

". . . Madam?"

The pharmacist was speaking to her. She had dark blond hair which jagged down stiffly at both sides of her face, in a way that told Jennifer right away that the girl used ceramic straighteners. She had deep black shadows beneath her eyes, and she was either flushed or someone had recently slapped her cheeks . . . maybe she'd slapped her cheeks herself in an attempt to stay awake here.

She was reading a magazine which lay before her, the pages tumbled open, one of her red-painted fingernails holding her place.

Jennifer attempted to comprehend the images within the magazine, but only succeeded in confusing her already tired mind —the mind which had been so switched on during the drive here, making sure that body obeyed every last traffic signal, every roundabout: right protocols, right—

". . . Are you okay, madam?" the girl / woman said.

Jennifer blinked away her confusion. She had been thinking about the magazines and how each of those images represented certain people who weren't here, like, *right now* . . . they were in other places, and yet, at the same time, in a sort of way, they were here too.

All of a sudden Jennifer snapped out of it.

Her mind came clear.

Because she knew how necessary this was . . . what she was doing.

She absolutely *needed* to fix just what had gone wrong.

Otherwise it absolutely *might* kill her.

And she could not allow her body to decay into nothingness, not yet, not now—

"Your nose," the girl / woman said, her eyes suddenly wide, apparently alarmed.

The girl might've done it subconsciously. Touched her dainty red-painted fingernails to her own nose so that Jennifer might better comprehend.

And when Jennifer aped her, when she touched the spot the girl indicated, and brought her fingers back for inspection, she found blood there. Seeping out of her nostril. She looked back to the girl. Wanted to tell her something. Wanted to *assure* her that everything was okay. But all that she could get out was a sort of low *moan.*

The girl / woman seemed to snap out of inaction. She rushed about, digging about beneath the counter of her pharmacy for something or other.

Soon, it turned out, she was scrabbling for cotton balls, and other assorted medical supplies.

Jennifer stood there—comparatively powerless—as the girl rounded the counter and worked at her face. Jennifer felt the soft material of the cotton balls up against her skin. And though the world was sharp, and pointed, and apparently keen to inflict harm upon her, she resisted the urge to break out into screaming, the urge to simply ball up her fists like some petulant toddler and rush back and forth, through the aisles, spilling everything onto the floor of this late-night pharmacy, her despair now too much for her to handle.

"Madam?" the girl said, this time sounding a little more highly strung. "Are you . . . uh, are you quite all right?"

Jennifer wanted to answer in the affirmative, but knew she didn't have the strength.

All she could do was hold out the plastic bottle, still tight in her grasp, sort of pass it towards the girl and hope that she might understand her voiceless communication.

But the girl only glanced at the bottle for a moment, and then returned her attention to stuffing up Jennifer's nose with the cotton balls.

"I'm gonna have to call an ambulance," she said. "The bleeding's not stopping."

Jennifer would've liked to say something else. Something to stop her from thinking what she was thinking, but the truth was that she could do nothing now.

Even she realised that on some deep, or maybe *gut*, level.

"Can you hold this?" the girl said, indicating the wads of cotton balls which she'd been clasping by the handful and pressing up against Jennifer's nostrils.

Jennifer realised right away that she wouldn't be able to hold the cotton balls both onto her bleeding nostrils *and* retain possession of the plastic bottle, so she decided to let the bottle go.

That didn't stop her watching the bottle tumble. Land with a *thunk-thunk* and then skittle off somewhere beneath the shelves. Lost forever. But, thankfully, empty.

She knew that bottle had nothing to offer her now.

She had, after all, arrived here.

To the pharmacy.

The girl disappeared off into some back room of the pharmacy and Jennifer was vaguely aware of hearing that plastic *clunk* of a phone being picked up.

Or maybe she just imagined it.

That was a possibility too.

Jennifer continued to hold the cotton balls up to her face. To her it felt like the bleeding was easing off, but, then again, she really was no expert.

All the same, she found that she had the strength—the strength to shift from where she was and to reach out, take hold of the pharmacy counter, to steady herself, and to ease her way around it.

There was a hinged flap that led through to the other side of the counter, and Jennifer managed to remove one of her hands holding the cotton balls to her nose, and to lift up the flap, to push it over to one side.

She was right where she wanted to be.

As she scanned the supplies, all laid out behind glass cases, she tried to see something that might catch her eye, something that would suggest to her that she was on the right track.

Because, if she was true to herself, she had to admit that she really had no idea what she was looking for.

Oh, she knew more or less the shape of the bottle, the pattern of the label, but she'd let go of the emptied one, allowed it to tumble down beneath the shelves and out of sight.

And the forgetting had begun.

Jennifer became increasingly aware of the girl, and where she might be.

She knew that she shouldn't be back here, but surely, if the girl had somehow understood her needs, then she would've comprehended just *why* she had to do this, and right now.

Jennifer felt her nose pulsing, and she could almost feel the blood weighing down the cotton balls as it rolled out from her. She worked faster. Scanned the labels and shapes faster. Tried to work out just where the medication she needed might be.

But still she saw nothing at all.

She reached the end of the counter which looked out onto the rest of the pharmacy, realised that she had looked through it all without luck.

That only left one option for her now.

Looking in the back room.

Going into the place where the girl had disappeared to.

Where she'd made the phone call.

But, before she got the chance, the girl re-emerged, face even more flushed now it seemed.

Jennifer half expected a reprimand, but the girl showed only concern.

"Oh," she said, with wide-open eyes. "It's still gushing hard." And then, "The ambulance will be here soon, don't worry—just a few minutes, that's what they said."

And then, as Jennifer's mind seemed to ebb in and out of this world, dipping its toe in the next, she felt a deep, deep . . . *profound* blackness overwhelm her.

Just like that, everything was gone.

8

T HE *BLEEP-BLEEP* of some machine brought her around.
Jennifer felt her heart throbbing low and gentle.

A dim sort of warmth bathed her.

When she managed to open her eyes, she saw that she was tucked into a hospital bed, one of those beds with beige plastic—or were they steel?—bars drawn up at the sides so she wouldn't tumble right on out in the middle of the night . . . or was this day?

It was difficult to tell with this ever-present, buzzing, and wildly *even* light all around.

And not a window in sight.

Her head throbbed. She had a stabbing sensation at her temples, like some invisible child stood at her bedside prodding at her.

Mocking her.

When she tried to sit up straight in her bed, the room began to spin, and she laid back once more. Not wanting to tempt fate, or anything like that.

The steady *bleep-bleep* went on a little more, and when she turned her head, she saw there was a machine beside her. A machine with a winking, neon-red light. She really didn't know what to make of it, and, thankfully for her, she soon heard the padding, muted footsteps of someone approaching.

When she glanced up, to the doorway of the room, she saw the doctor there.

He was presented to her by the hospital-green shade of the doorframe. He had tufty brown hair, and rich, chocolate eyes which sheened from behind his round spectacles.

He wore a white coat and grasped hold of a clipboard.

Reminding Jennifer of those scammy men who'd come to call.

"Mrs Douglas?" the doctor said, his voice a little raspy—but in a way she quite liked.

She saw that he had tanned skin to go with that sharp accent of his too, and she wondered if he might be South American.

"Hmm?" she said, her head feeling bleary, and far too sharp for her liking.

"How are you feeling?"

"Oh," she said, remembering herself, and the plasticky sheets which were tucked in all around her. "Just fine."

He gave her a resilient smile then allowed his clipboard to fall down to his waist.

Now she saw, looking properly at the clipboard once again, that it wasn't a clipboard at all—no, it was one of those new-style computer tablets.

Much handier.

Much more modern.

"Would you like some light?" he said.

For a second, Jennifer was confused by the question, and then she realised that he meant *day*light. She thought about it for a moment, and then gave a nod of her head.

That sent nausea plunging down to the pit of her stomach, and she had to make an effort to fight back against the taste of bile at the back of her throat.

She watched on as the doctor confidently strode across the room—across the greeny-brown, waxed floor—and over to the window.

She saw now that it was one of those black-out blinds.

The blinds that snuffed out the vaguest suggestion of sunrays.

With a nimble motion, he jerked hard on the plastic, bobbly cord, and she watched the blind whip upwards. Spin about as it rolled about itself. Sunlight flowed in through the window, and

Jennifer could see the expansive blue skies stretching all the way to the horizon.

Somewhere—too—she was fairly certain she could hear that same, slightly *smug*, bird twittering and chirping.

She looked back to the doctor who now stood with his back to the window and his arms folded across his chest. The computer tablet dangling down from his fingertips, threatening to drop if Jennifer hadn't been so thoroughly convinced of this man's dexterity and strength.

"Is that better?" he said, again with a smile in his voice.

She nodded.

He nodded back, then she observed a few wrinkles form about his eyes as he was apparently turning to serious matters. "Mrs Douglas," he said. "We brought you in here after you had your fall, do you remember?"

Jennifer stretched her mind. Thought back to those *pharmacy* smells . . . and those aisles and aisles of things in blue and white packages . . . but none of them what she'd been looking for . . . what *had* she been looking for?

She gave him another nod in reply.

His smile thickened a little and it made her think that, maybe, she'd given him the right answer. He adjusted his spectacles over the bridge of his heavy, large nose—back into the blood-red notches he had in his skin there. "While you were unconscious, we ran a few tests." He paused for a long moment and Jennifer wondered if he might've lost his train of thought. That happened to her from time to time. But then, just when she was wondering if she should respond in some way, he continued. "Is there anything you'd like to tell us, Mrs Douglas?"

Again, Jennifer tried hard to remember. Tried to *think back* to the pharmacy.

What *had* she been doing there?

. . . And why had she fallen?

After what must've been a solid half a minute of thought, and all the time with that blithering birdsong chirruping about outside the window, she shook her head.

She observed the slight twitch in the doctor's eye, and she was left in no doubt that, this time, she had surely given the wrong answer.

The doctor adjusted his spectacles again. Coughed once. Twice. Then he unfolded his arms and tapped at his tablet computer. He coughed another time, using his fist to suppress his mouth, and then he glanced back at her. "We've found a, uh, *substance* in your blood."

When Jennifer answered him, her words felt faraway, kind of *floaty.* ". . . A substance?" she said.

"Hmm, yes, a prescribed substance, which is to say that it is a substance *only* available with a prescription." He paused again. Tapped the screen of his computer tablet, and then went on, as if he was reading off notes from there. "However, the levels of this *substance* within your blood was far, *far*"—when he said that he met her eye over the rim of the computer tablet—"above the acceptable levels."

"Oh," Jennifer replied.

"Yes," the doctor said, crossing his arms again, the tablet apparently not of use for the time being.

Jennifer attempted to make sense of this.

What was he talking about some . . . some *substance?*

Surely she would've remembered it.

Or would she?

The doctor gave her a thin-lipped smile then said, "Don't worry, we have a programme which we are looking to have you signed up for—however, I only wished to come here and to see whether you might have any, uh, *useful* information to add to our speculations?"

Again, Jennifer thought long and hard.

A programme?

What on Earth did he mean?

She strained her brain a little more, and then, right there from the back somewhere, like a student on the last row of a classroom vigorously waving their hand to volunteer an answer, it came to her.

Yes . . . yes, now she had it . . . and though she could feel her brain squidging up, like an over-soaked sponge, she found that she could remember.

Found her memories coming back to her.

Thick and fast.

She looked to the doctor, eyebrows raised. "Will you help me, doctor?"

The doctor smiled a little wider, and then gave her a firm nod.

9

T HROUGHOUT her week-long stay at *Heelsmorth's Medical Institute*—the private clinic she'd awoken in, which, it turned out, was covered by her *extremely* comprehensive insurance —she couldn't help but think back, think back to her house, and to those white plastic bottles, and wonder just how things had got so bad.

She talked things through with the people there—the people who wanted to *help*—and she did her best to be honest. To give them the answers they required.

It was funny how things played out.

As if she was a kind of willing partner in the investigation of her past self.

They established facts.

Each breakthrough surprised Jennifer as much as it did the staff.

The prescriptions, it turned out, had been forged many times over by Jennifer herself. She had gone to different pharmacies each time to get her fix—to get the bottle of stuff that would keep her ticking.

And she couldn't help but feel the sting of shame as she turned the facts over in her mind.

She was a modern woman what with a house of her own that she *owned* herself—one hundred percent, no bank necessary. And, as they continued to investigate her past self, she discovered she had once been a high-flying . . . or at least a *lucrative* . . . accountant.

Where it had all unravelled, it was tricky to say.

There were no clues.

Not from where they sat, in the clinic.

She would need to go *home* for *those* clues.

It was odd how each day came clearer than the previous one and how, when she'd least expected it, one of the members of staff proposed that she was well enough to go home—and gave her only a laminated business card with a number to call if she found herself getting into any trouble at all . . . getting those same old *familiar* cravings.

Though she couldn't see why she would.

As she emerged outside, dressed in fresh clothes she'd had brought to her—a smart, light-purple trouser suit as befitted a lady of her standing, and matching shoes—she felt the sun on her back, streaming up against her cheeks, warming her blood up.

Making her feel alive.

Because it was just like she'd come back alive once again.

Like she'd woken up after a deep—and *cleansing*—sleep.

The taxi waiting on the curb whisked her home at double time, or so it seemed, and before Jennifer knew it, she was standing back on her front doorstep, key in hand, shaking almost uncontrollably.

Because beyond that door was her past self.

Ghosts haunted this house.

A ghost of *herself* among them.

And yet, she knew she had to take the first step.

Else she would never recover.

That was the hardest part.

The stepping in through the door.

But she managed it.

And before she knew it, she was standing in her front hall, on the Welcome mat, where she had greeted—if that *truly* was the right word—those men who had come to scam her . . . had they been scammers at all, or simply normal working men looking to do their job.

As if some higher power confirmed this to her, she found the envelope on the Welcome mat. One of those with the cheap brown *flimsy* paper. Holding the envelope up to the light, she could almost make out the contents of it. Could almost make out the letters written on the folded-up paper snuggled within.

Only one word mattered, though, the one that said 'solicitor'.

She would deal with *that* later on . . .

She left the envelope on the kitchen counter and strolled on through the rest of the house.

Though she didn't quite gather as much consciously at the time, she finally did realise that she was *searching*—that she was looking for *something* . . . the *something* that had set her off in the first place, that had seen her spiral down into *that* pit of despair.

After an hour of scouring the house, she found nothing at all.

Not till she reached the sitting room.

Approached the polished walnut desk there.

It was in the third drawer down on the right-hand side.

A picture frame.

A picture inside it.

She felt the air leaving her lungs—a strange lightness taking over her bones, making it seem like they were no more substantial than kindling.

She took one step back.

Two.

Felt for the wall behind her.

Found it.

Sure.

Secure.

Right there and waiting for her.

All over she was trembling and some force of gut led her away from the desk—away from that *drawer* . . . away from that *photograph* . . .

Before she even knew where she was going herself, she found herself standing back in her kitchen, headed for the walk-in pantry, and then surrounding herself with the coolness, and the regimented tin cans standing to attention on the shelves.

When she breathed in, the air had a flavour of cardboard to it—that kind of tasteless, paper-like smell. But that wasn't what she was looking for. No. She knew just what awaited her here . . . in the pantry.

Down there, on the floor, towards the back of a trio of bottles of olive oil, she spotted it.

That white plastic bottle.

Another one.

One which had, *obviously*, slipped her mind.

But she saw it right now.

And that was all that mattered.

She didn't open the bottle right away. She had *enough* self-control to prevent her from doing that. What with all the tips she'd got from the staff of the clinic she was certain she would be able to see this through alone, that she would be able to exercise restraint.

She paced through her house, over the thick carpets, and towards the patio doors. The doors which looked on out into her verdant—if slightly overgrown—garden.

The lock was so simple to open, just a matter of twisting the key.

The mechanism making a slight *click*.

And just like that the fresh spring breeze blew up against her.

Caught her hair, and blew it back onto her neck.

Birdsong filled the summer afternoon air.

And Jennifer couldn't help but feel positive.

Positive about the world ahead of her.

Leaving the decisions she had made behind.

Because now she knew . . . she had the benefit of perspective, knew just why she had gone and turned out the way she had done.

How she had pushed things too far.

But, as she allowed herself to bend at the knees, and to sit herself down on the white-painted wooden doorstep which looked out over her garden, she knew that the same wouldn't happen again.

Not this time.

She promised *that* to herself.

And, with that thought thick in her mind, she pushed hard down on the safety cap of the plastic bottle—*twisted* hard—and listened to the gentle *hiss* as the trapped air escaped.

That milky smell came back to her.

She felt her tongue immediately bathed in saliva.

Her heart beat a little harder.

Her blood ran a little warmer.

And, all at once, she knew that she'd come home.

Come home for good.

WHY PIGS DON'T FLY

THE PLANE ENGINES droned on long and hard, and Phillip couldn't help but stare out through the oval window, into the bright, white mass of cloud passing by. He wished he could be somewhere else—*anywhere* else.

Phillip brushed a piece of lint from the leg of his suit trousers, and he shook his head to himself at the idiocy of the bods behind arranging this particular meeting. A meeting in a particular city which meant Phillip taking *this* particular flight . . . the *only* feasible flight, and one which required him to be fully dressed for said meeting, and to leave the airport and go right to said meeting before turning around and coming back home.

It was enough to make a chap want to sigh.

When he had checked in for the flight, Phillip has *specifically* informed the airline employee, as he always did, that he would sit anywhere—*absolutely anywhere*—on the plane just as long as he wasn't seated beside a child. And look what had happened.

He'd been sat beside a *child*.

Now, it was fair to say that this particular child was well-behaved.

It neither puked or whined, neither had it attempted any sort of a conversation with Phillip.

As far as children went, Phillip had to admit that this particular child was somewhere near the top of the rotten barrel.

If he'd had to guess at the child's age, Phillip would've said that he was around nine or ten, but Phillip's guess—as he well knew—was worth precisely jackshit.

He made it his life's work to stay out of children's way.

But now it had happened.

This *child* had happened.

What was annoying Phillip about the child wasn't the fact that the child was reading, or that he was silently mouthing along the words he read.

Though it would've been understandable.

No, the fact was that this *particular* child was reading a book with a pig flying on the cover. And this wasn't anything easily explained. It wasn't like the pig on the front cover of the kid's book was wearing a helmet having been freshly shot out of some circus canon. And neither was it that said pig had—*somehow*—sprouted a pair of wings and simply 'taken to the skies'.

Nope, nope, nope.

This pig had achieved flight without any obvious propulsion mechanism that Phillip could divine. The pig was simply *gliding* through the sky.

Phillip had attempted to get his head around this—around *this* phenomenon—but he had come up short. *Way, way short.* And he'd come to the conclusion that the only way to get to the bottom of this fanciful *lie*—because what was fiction but *lies?*—would be to indulge the child in conversation.

And so Phillip did, albeit cautiously.

"Excuse me?" Phillip said.

The child, who was wearing a light-blue shirt and a pair of chequered shorts which ended just before his knees glanced up over his book at Phillip. He said nothing, but it was clear that Phillip had his attention . . . that was only a matter of time, though, for where *children* were concerned, he knew that they only had a gnat's attention span.

"That pig," Phillip said, deciding to get right to it. "On the front cover, how does it fly?"

The child remained still. He cocked his head to one side, and for a long moment, Phillip was sure that he was going to be accosted by the child's parents. Because, in this day and age, simply *speaking* to somebody else's child could easily get you some wicked looks.

"Just does," the child finally answered, and then looked past Phillip, casually out the window, and returned his full attention to his book.

Phillip stewed in silence for a long few seconds.

Although he really had no interest in continuing the conversation, he caught a tickling sensation in the base of his gut which sort of demanded that he follow this up.

To put this child right.

It was for the boy's own good.

"Look here," Phillip said, "there're several solidly founded scientific, technological—and dare I say it—*philosophical* reasons why a pig cannot fly by its own means."

The boy stared at Phillip over the top of his book. His mouth latched open slightly.

"For a start *take-off*," Phillip said, "How on *earth* would a pig be able to generate thrust—let alone *lift*—using its own means, hmm?"

The boy remained blank.

Mouth still latched open.

It didn't matter, the boy had to understand.

"And let us assume that this *pig* does manage to achieve flight—and let us make no bones about it, that *would* be a magnificent achievement—just how would it manage to stay airborne do you think?"

Phillip awaited his answer, but got none.

He continued on, unabated, "And taking all that into consideration, and scratching off those insurmountable obstacles as mere *bagatelles*, then how would the pig manage to return to the ground? How would it manage to bring its velocity down to a suitable level for landing, hmm?"

The boy remained motionless for another few moments. His mouth still latched open.

Phillip thought about going on, but it was pointless, really. He had already made this boy understand, or at least he had tried his best. He reached into the pocket in front of him and he removed the inflight magazine. He leafed through the colourful, glossy pages, but could find nothing of *substance* to concentrate on.

It was only a couple of minutes later, when Phillip had forgotten the conversation—or else tried his best to do so—when the boy sparked up.

"It's just magic, mister, no need to get upset about it."

Phillip sat very still in his seat, and when he looked back at the boy, he saw that he was buried back in that *gunk* of his . . . back to reading about flying pigs, and whoever knew what else. It was experiences like these that made Phillip glad he had never had children.

He could hardly *imagine* how they might've turned out.

GOTTA HAVE CLEAN TEETH

1

OFTEN KARLSON DAVIS—lead singer of *Cut the Mop*—felt bad about the way they exploited their bass player, Paul. But, at the end of it all, he supposed the guy brought it on himself.

He was the one who shot the stuff up his arm.

The one who made all his own decisions.

Things for which Paul, and only Paul, was responsible.

Still, Karlson wondered if they should bring this whole farce to a natural end at some point. Not quite yet, though. Not quite yet.

Karlson snuck through the darkened area of backstage. He felt the velvet, dusty curtains brush up against his skin. When he breathed in, he could feel the dust layering onto the back of his throat, and making him want to sneeze. His heart beat harder —*faster*—and he felt almost like somebody might be watching him; somewhere, somehow.

He still had the slightly sour aftertaste of beer on his tongue.

His pre-show routine.

Karlson emerged at the side of the stage: all dressed in what his girlfriend termed his 'flowery pirate shirt;' a lilac-coloured affair with those dangly bits about the front that he never recalled the name of. He could still smell his girlfriend's scent. That slight odour of men's deodorant, which she insisted on using, which she, for some reason, believed to be more effective than the female equivalent.

He found himself in silent company there, at the side of the stage.

A sound engineer.

A roadie or two.

They nodded to him in the darkness.

The sudden silence had fallen across the whole audience now.

And Karlson knew that the show was about to start.

Karlson turned his attention onto the darkened stage. It was almost as if he controlled things with a single twitch of the eye. Like he'd given some silent signal to somebody watching on—like he had brought about the commencement of proceedings.

The spotlight blinked on.

It illuminated a small, white circle in the centre of the stage.

A battered, old armchair which they'd hurriedly acquired from some charity shop down the road. Though it was tricky to tell in the incredibly bright light, it was a beige colour—that colour which seemed to have been all the rage back in the seventies—and had stuffing bursting from its seams.

Karlson recalled, back in the shop, the stuffing had been this grim, nuclear-yellow colour, and he'd actually been afraid to touch it. He hadn't spent much attention on all that physics stuff back at school—or had it been chemistry?—and so he didn't really know the ins and outs of the thing. One thing he did know, though, was that if you got yourself too close to something radioactive, you were liable to get killed.

And Karlson didn't *want* to die.

Not when he still had so much to do.

So much to *give* the world.

He turned his attention back to the stage.

To that battered armchair in the centre.

And to his bass guitarist—Paul—slumped up on it, his feet dangling over one of the arms.

Karlson's chest tightened. The aftertaste of beer got drier still in his mouth. He could hear the chatter among the audience begin to strike up once more.

They'd come here for the show.

To be *entertained.*

And that was what they expected right now.

As if they'd disturbed his sleep, Paul raised his head up to examine them. He squinted in the harsh spotlight. He was taking them in slowly. Taking them in *ever* so slowly. And Karlson couldn't help wondering if things were going to work out tonight.

If this was *truly* going to go just like it had the night before.

At the last show.

The problem had come when their support act: *Violent Acts of Passion,* had pulled out at the last moment the night before. With no time to find another support act, Karlson had had the idea of just grabbing their bass player Paul and shoving him the hell out there on the stage. How should Karlson have known that Paul still grasped his toothbrush in his fist, or that he'd only recently stuck a needle in his arm, or snorted something, or chewed on this thing, or some other thing?

But it had certainly been a spectacle.

Of that there'd been no doubt.

And so Karlson and the rest of the band had determined to try the whole routine once more.

Tonight.

On *this* unsuspecting audience.

The armchair had just been a whim. While they'd been flurrying through the centre of town in their tour bus, Karlson had caught sight of the furniture all nestled within the charity shop window, and he had made them stop. They'd got off. And agreed a decent price for the armchair. It had nearly been free . . . Karlson tended to be a little more conservative when it came to money management, as compared to the rest of the band.

Karlson felt a slight shudder pass through him. It was almost as if the darkness of the backstage area, right where he stood, pressed up against his skin. The best way he had ever been able to describe it to himself, was like he was passing through a massive group of black bears. Brushing up against their fur. Feeling their warmth. And yet ready, at any moment, for one of them to bite him clean across the throat.

On the centre of the stage, Karlson observed his bandmate, Paul, rising up out of the armchair. He seemed a touch beleaguered by the brightness of the spotlight. He brought his arm up to shield his eyes. He took a step forwards.

Another.

From the audience, Karlson could hear the nervous mutterings.

People didn't know what to make of this spectacle.

They had expected some young rock-and-roll upstarts—some *younger* rock-and-roll upstarts. They hadn't thought that they would come here to experience some sort of a performance-art project. And though Karlson found himself screwing up his eyes even to *think* that that was a term which could be used to describe what was going on here, he couldn't think of another adequate way to describe the sight.

Karlson turned his attention to Paul's hands, to what he held tight in his fist.

The toothbrush.

2

KARLSON COULD FEEL some movement over his shoulder.

When he looked back, he saw that it was Linda—his girlfriend.

She gave him a slight smile and sidled up beside him. He felt a warm glow emanate out from her skin. That was how she always got after a few beers. It seemed to bring all her veins to the surface.

Karlson draped his arm lightly about her shoulders.

He felt her lips lightly rub against his earlobe.

"Do you think this is right?" she said, in a whisper. "I mean, to be doing this?"

Karlson gave her a little squeeze. He said nothing in reply.

Because he could think of nothing to say.

He turned his attention back to the stage.

Paul was dressed in his signature all-denim outfit: from his waistcoat with nothing on underneath, to his jeans on the bottom, and those clumpy boots he'd seemed to have had forever, and which Karlson imagined he'd picked up from some Army-surplus store.

Paul held tight to his toothbrush.

Karlson could see how a little gob of toothpaste continued to stick to it. A couple of droplets dripped down and splattered onto the wooden floorboards of the stage.

One of the droplets struck Paul's boot.

Karlson could feel the extreme concentration of the audience—how they all seemed to stare right at Paul, waiting for him to get to the point, if there was a point to be got at. Some of the members of the audience were pointing at the toothbrush Paul held, some of them were shaking their head.

Nobody had a clue what was going on.

Karlson allowed himself a wry smile.

That was just the thing.

The whole point.

He *wanted* the audience to be confused.

Slowly—so gradually, as if what Paul held wasn't only a tooth-brush, but something so delicate as a bird's nest—Paul brought the toothbrush up to his lips. He parted his mouth and prodded the toothbrush inside.

And then he began to brush.

First gentle strokes.

And then tougher ones.

Karlson watched the audience's transfixed expressions.

Even from where Karlson stood, here, at the side of the stage, he was sure that he could smell the gentle peppermint of the toothpaste. He felt a slight tremble in his gut. For the briefest of seconds, he imagined that he might be standing there in Paul's position.

In his *boots*.

Looking out over the audience.

And Karlson had to remind himself that he was, in fact, only an observer.

Here at the side of the stage.

Paul continued his brushing. The way that the toothpaste had lathered, it spewed forth from his lips now, making Paul appear almost as if he was some sort of a rabid dog. Toothpaste was dribbling down his chin, onto his denim waistcoat. And it was splattering onto the wooden floorboards at his feet.

For some reason, Karlson wished for the toothpaste to land on one of the audience members.

Would that involve them to some greater extent?

Or would it be far too much for them to take?

There would be only one way to find out.

Karlson felt Linda tugging on his shirt sleeve. He glanced at her, and he saw that she was shaking her head. She wanted this over with. It was scaring her. That much was certain. And yet Karlson knew that they couldn't stop. That they had to keep going with this.

That it was important for the show.

It made the show *stronger*.

Karlson turned his attention back to the stage.

Paul was still brushing away at his teeth with great vigour.

There was no sign of him stopping when, all of a sudden, he did.

He just ceased his jigging movements.

Stopped dead in his brushing.

Karlson could see Paul's face in profile, and he knew that he had a whole mouthful of toothpaste. Perhaps he no longer had any space remaining to brush. Maybe he needed to spit.

That could be it.

That *certainly* could be it.

Paul turned his gaze onto the audience. He breathed in deeply, through his nostrils. His shoulders arched back, and he seemed to puff upwards so that he was several times the size he had been before. And then, parting his lips—a tiny way at first, and then further—he began the mumblings.

What Karlson would later identify as the ramblings of a madman.

Karlson had attempted to listen to the words. Maybe it was the lead-singer part of him that had wanted to do that. He had wanted to distinguish just exactly what was being said. That was why he spent so long off at the side of the stage, not wanting to leave his spot.

Little did he know that only a matter of seconds later he would hear those words loud and clear, and impossible to miss.

All the same, it began at the level of a whisper—a volume which, Karlson was certain, even those at the front row of the show would've struggled to hear.

Indeed, at first, Karlson only caught the odd word.

"... Gotta ... Teeth ... Have ... Clean ..."

Karlson could still feel Linda tugging at his shirt sleeve, and he shook her off with a single jerk of his arm. He stared on at Paul at the same time knowing what he was seeing—and yet, also knowing that he could do nothing to prevent this.

The words were clear now.

A refrain.

Almost like some sort of a mantra.

"Gotta have clean teeth, gotta have clean teeth, gotta have clean teeth."

Over and over again.

No stopping.

"Gotta have clean teeth, gotta have ... gotta have ..."

Nobody touched Karlson now, and he really had little idea what he should do. Should he shift from his place? Step onto the stage? Stop this?

Paul continued to gnash his teeth at the audience. The foam spilled down his chin. It dampened the front of his denim waistcoat. But he wouldn't stop. He would continue like this forever if nobody stepped in.

It was then that Karlson felt his girlfriend Linda's nudge in his back, and he took it as his cue to step onto the stage. He felt strange. He was so used to feeling the whole of the audience's gaze on him—tracking his *every* movement—but, right now, they were all fixed on Paul the bass player.

Transfixed.

Unable to look away.

Karlson was careful in his approach. He didn't want to trigger anything from Paul. He didn't want to come across as a sort of threat to him. So he reached up and, ever so carefully, laid his arm about Paul's shoulders.

Paul was amenable to his touch, and when Karlson edged him towards the side of the stage, Paul came with him. But he kept uttering those words, and the toothpaste continued to dribble down his chin.

"Gotta have clean teeth . . . gotta *have* clean teeth!"

3

IN THE GREEN ROOM, backstage, the rest of the band: Karlson's drummer, Fredrick, and his guitarist, Molly, were all shaken up by what had happened to Paul; at how those men had come along to take him away. And how they'd talked about sedation and restraints—and how Karlson had only just managed to convince them that such measures would not be necessary.

But Karlson had no real way of knowing what would happen once they had taken Paul out of his sight.

The green room, just like all green rooms, looked like it'd been hit by a bomb sometime in the past, and nobody had bothered to piece it together again.

A series of emptied bottles all stood up on a rickety wooden table. The wooden table, Karlson knew, from experience, wouldn't withstand much more than a little gentle leaning before it collapsed. He could still smell the stale odour of beer, but Karlson didn't believe that it was the result of his band being here. He supposed that, over the years, the use and *abuse* of the place had brought about that stench.

Outside, along the corridor, Karlson could hear the audience getting restless.

He knew how different an audience might take something once the houselights came up. Those houselights had the power to transform a person. They would be concerned, of course they would.

And who was Karlson kidding?

He and the band were just as shaken up by what had happened as everybody else here.

And yet Karlson supposed he should've anticipated the thing.

What *had* he expected?

They were already about fifteen minutes late going on when Karlson finally reached the decision that he would have to go out there alone. And so, feeling almost like a battle-hardened warrior, he glanced about the others, and then snatched up his acoustic guitar—the one which'd been lying off in a case, half-forgotten amongst the rest of the gear.

He didn't even bother to see if the thing was in tune before stepping out onto the stage.

Feeling the harsh spotlight glaring down on him.

And, in that moment, feeling its warmth, the light rushing over him, he could somehow understand just how Paul might've felt.

Madness?

Was that the name for it?

NOBODY THINKS ABOUT
FACTORIES

1

A N ENDING was just a synonym for a beginning.
Yes, that was a quote worth keeping in mind.

Joan had heard that one from her grandmother, all that time ago, back when she'd been a little girl, in summer dresses, with her knee socks pulled *way* up, back when happiness had been fairly rigidly defined as running through fields of long grasses, and bathing naked in freshly running streams.

Thinking about it now, though, as she swished through the party between the penguin suits and the cocktail dresses, that saying seemed like a million miles away.

Quite simply put, what she was about to do felt *very far* from a beginning, in fact it felt more like the end of her life.

The party in question was the Patricks' annual fundraiser at Squoremyre Hall: for want of a better word, Joan's *home*.

Joan squared her shoulders, and she breathed in the choking perfumes and colognes that seemed to sweat off the guests. The smell of champagne cut through the air as sharp as a diamond, and seemed to cause those odours to take on an even more *dangerous* edge.

She got herself out of the main reception area, where a pianist tinkled away at some sort of a classical score—music had always escaped her—and where a line of girls, replete with feather boas, pranced about on the stage.

This was all just, well, *classless*.

No taste at all.

Nothing like what she had signed up for.

Back when she'd first met Richard Albermonz it had been all quick passions and fleeting pleasures: the backseats of limousines, the cushioned living areas of yachts, cosy chalets in the Alps. But, soon . . . well, if not *soon* exactly, then 'not too late' . . . Joan realised that all of those *nice* things were really just a façade.

A neat, prim, well-constructed façade.

But a façade, nonetheless.

When she reached Richard's home office, on the first floor of the Hall, she rapped the standard two times, and then waited for the grunted order for her to come in.

Richard's office had an enormous, mahogany desk which would've occupied another—*less expansive*—office. The book-shelves were stuffed to bursting with sun-faded hardbacks, but Joan knew the truth, that Richard abhorred reading, that to him it was 'boring'.

But, then again, just about everything that wasn't either alcohol or sex or money was boring to Richard.

Despite the seriousness of the situation, and how neatly she'd made her mind up, Joan almost smiled at her curt observation of her husband.

She had struck the proverbial nail on the head.

Richard had his back to her, looking out through the enormous window, out across the grounds of the Hall, all of the trees and the garden path lit up with an icy silver glow. As she followed Richard's gaze, she saw that he was focussed on the couple who were unceremoniously *screwing* on the lawn.

As if observing some fine art in a gallery, Richard simply brought his glass of—unwatered-down—whisky up to his lips and took a sip.

He didn't look back at her.

Not once.

He'd stopped looking at her about a year ago.

Joan gently shifted her way around to his side. Looked at him in profile. She took in his features, how they'd become grizzled by greying stubble. Despite being into his fifties, and being a large-framed, *tall* man, he didn't have a scrap of fat on him.

He looked just as muscular, just as well-kept as he had when Joan had first met him five years ago.

Five years . . . it seemed almost like an eternity, had it *really* been that long?

She thought back to who she'd been then, a naïve girl in her late twenties, pulse pounding, clock ticking, all her friends taking men off the market.

She had sworn that she would never be like them, that she would never act with the desperation she felt that her friends showed in wanting to 'settle down'.

And yet, look at her here, wasn't that exactly what she'd done?

. . . Well, to be fair to herself, she hadn't had any kids yet, and she couldn't exactly say that she'd met any sort of a soul mate. Her relationship with Richard was based on lust—even now—not *love*.

Richard took another sip of his whisky and then he slipped her a sidelong glance. He didn't smile, or grimace, or react in any way to her presence there. As he brought his glass back down level with his chest, he returned his attention to the couple on the lawn.

"What do you want?" he said.

Joan felt her chest tighten. Her arms all of a sudden felt flimsy. She was light-headed even though she'd had nothing at all to drink tonight—hadn't *dared* have anything to drink.

She supposed there was no point in beating about the bush.

"I want a divorce," she said.

Richard made no sound. No reaction at all. He continued to stare out through the cool glass, out onto the lawn, down onto that couple.

Joan wondered if he'd heard her at all.

She could still hear the light *burble* of chatter floating in beneath the door to Richard's office, the rest of their guests all enjoying their time here, this evening. She breathed in hard, at the same time taking in Richard's thick, musky scent, feeling it dry out her throat.

She turned her mind back onto the matter at hand.

She had to keep her focus.

Keep her eyes on just what she wanted.

What she *needed*.

"It's not working, Richard," she said. "It hasn't been working for some time, you must know that."

Richard, again, brought his whisky up to his lips and drank. "Have you been planning this?" he said, still not looking at her.

"What?" Joan said, a little stunned at the hard tone to his voice.

Richard flapped his spare hand, the hand not holding the tumbler of whisky. "*All* of this! You know, wanting to bide your time, make a spectacle"—this time he *did* turn to look at her, giving her both barrels of those black eyes of his—"*embarrass* me?"

" 'Embarrass' you?" Joan said, meeting his gaze, feeling her forehead crinkle.

"Yes, you know that I'm speaking sense, why else would you wait for a big occasion like this, wait till we've got the house totally full to pack your bags?"

Strangely, Joan found herself almost spluttering on a laugh. "You think that I'm going *right now?*"

Richard didn't reply.

"You think that, *really*, this is all about you, that I've got all my bags waiting outside my bedroom, ready to carry them down through the drawing room, through all the guests, so that everybody can see?"

No response from Richard.

"Do you really think that I'm such a drama queen?"

There was a long, pregnant silence between the two of them.

Joan could see that Richard only had a slop of whisky remaining in the base of his tumbler, and she knew that he longed to head over to his drinks cabinet in the corner for a refill. And he would as soon as she'd left.

But he hadn't got shot of her.

Not yet.

When Richard spoke again his tone was impossibly calm and collected. It was a tone that infuriated Joan, that made her see stars. She wished that just, for once, he would show some sort of emotion that hadn't already been passed through some internal filter. "Your bags are already waiting," he said. "Outside your room. Ready for you to leave."

The gasp died in Joan's throat, but she managed to get out, "*Richard?*"

"I won't have somebody living under *my* roof who does not wish to be around me, that's all that there is to be said."

Joan blinked away her temporary surprise. "Won't you give me until the morning?"

Richard shook his head and then he knocked back the rest of his glass of whisky. He held the glass so tightly in his fist that Joan was afraid, for a couple of seconds, that it might break.

When she followed his gaze this time, she saw that he was no longer looking out the window at the couple fornicating but into some spot in mid-air that was invisible, at least, to her. She knew from Richard's moods that this was her chance to get away.

To break free.

And there was no way that she would pass it up.

She shifted away from Richard's side, got herself out past the thick, oak door, and then she stood outside on the landing for a couple of moments.

About ten seconds later, she heard a loud *grunt* followed by the *tinkling* of breaking glass.

Richard tossing his tumbler across the room, into the wall, just as she had seen him do so many times before.

Yes, she was decided, this was for the best.

2

I T WASN'T TILL the next night that Joan felt anything at all. Anything besides numbness.

Just like Richard had asked, the night before she had lugged her bags out of the house, past the gawping guests, making that spectacle that Richard had so craved, and she had slumped herself into the waiting car.

Then she'd been driven to this hotel where she sat now—the penthouse suite—which had already been paid for by Richard.

Though the moment the driver had set off without her so much as needing to give him an address, she had known that they were headed for a destination handpicked by Richard, she hadn't seen any way that she might be able to avoid it.

After all, these five years of marriage she had lived as a kept woman.

It was funny how, after those first *intense* few months of being with Richard had become her everyday reality, she had slipped into the lifestyle so easily.

Before she had had her morals.

Her life goals.

Her own career aspirations.

But, one by one, Richard had stolen those from her.

Left her with only copies of his credit and debit cards and now *this*: a penthouse suite in a hotel with a French name.

The simple truth was that, if she left this penthouse, if she set out on her lonesome, she knew that Richard would block her accounts, leave her without a penny. And, anyway, where would she run to? She had no family left. Her 'friends', as far as they went, all occupied Richard's sphere, had all, thinking about it, come to her through his influence.

No, though she had left the Hall, she was under no illusions that she was striking out on her own. Not at all. Not yet. If she truly wanted independence then she would have to strive for it. She would have to *work hard*.

There had been a time when she had *wanted* to work hard, when it had seemed the most satisfactory of ways for her to accomplish her wishes. Make all her dreams come true.

Why, oh *why*, had she allowed them to dissolve so quickly after Richard had arrived into her life?

She sat up at a window seat with the cushions all plumped up about her. She stared down into the street, at the lazy Sunday morning cars as they trundled about the deserted roads. She opened the window just a little, allowed the fresh morning air into the suite. She could still smell all the colognes and perfumes of the guests from the Hall from the night before, and, when she breathed especially deep, she caught a whiff of whisky and musk: Richard.

Already now she was regretting what she'd done.

Trying to work out how she might be able to go back in time.

Not have *said* what she had.

But the fact remained, thinking about it more, that Richard had apparently known for as long as she had that they were on the cusp of breakdown, that they were heading for divorce.

He had already had her bags packed.

Had the car waiting.

Was she really so predictable?

There was a knock at the door to the penthouse suite.

For a long couple of moments, Joan hoped that it had just been a dream, and that, really, there wasn't anybody who wanted to speak with her. She just wanted to be alone. To think her own thoughts. She had spent so much of the past five years being a conduit—simply allowing the thoughts and opinions of others to tumble through her. That had been her role. To be Richard's eye candy. It was good to have time to think.

There was another knock, this time louder.

With a long-won weariness, Joan lifted herself up off the window cushions and she slipped her feet back into the leather-strapped sandals which Richard would never have allowed her to wear in company . . . let alone to answer the door.

When she answered the caller, she saw that it was a man of about thirty years old—about her age. He wore a smart suit with a crisp cut and a light-pink shirt underneath. He didn't wear a tie.

As she finished up her analysis of his dress, she moved onto his features. To his black hair, and his *clean* blue eyes. He had a strong nose, one of those *dependable* noses, and his chin jutted down in a way that put Joan in mind of an exclamation mark.

"Yes?" Joan said.

The man smiled at her, revealing perfect, pearly teeth. "Mrs Albermonz?"

Though Joan felt a slight twang at the base of her stomach just from hearing *his* name, she nodded.

"I wanted to come and speak with you this morning because I believe I have a proposal that might interest you."

Joan's mind, somehow, flashed back onto a track long-ago taught her by Richard. She remembered how he had given her a talk about taking care with her . . . *his* money. That there were 'vultures', as he termed them, who were very much tuned into the fact that she had access to sizeable bank accounts. While she'd thought his chat extremely *condescending* at the time, now she saw how easily she might've been fooled. Look at her now, standing here, at her most vulnerable . . . she might well have agreed to this man, might've continued her conversation with him . . . might've spent all the money resting in her account if Richard hadn't had the fore-sight to block her accounts already.

Her gut instinct told her that he already had.

She made to close the door, but the man was quick, and he managed to jam his foot in the crack before she got a chance to close it.

Never before had Joan found herself *preparing* to scream, but she certainly did so now.

She even had the presence of mind to recall that she had to scream 'fire!' rather than 'help!' so that people would actually pay some attention.

But she didn't have a chance to get out so much as a *squeak*, because the man lurched forwards, grabbed her from behind and held his hand over her mouth.

Joan struggled for several seconds till it became evident that he had far too much strength for her. So she opted to save her strength. She went limp and bided her time, her eyes falling onto his.

With a neat back-heel, the man shut the door to the penthouse suite.

When he spoke again, his voice was calm, *collected*, "I'm going to let you go, Mrs Albermonz, okay? But you've got to promise that you won't scream."

Joan told herself that she would do the exact opposite of what this man asked.

That the second he removed his hand from her mouth she would let loose a blood-curdling scream—a scream that'd bring half of the police force running.

She held herself still.

"Do I have you word?" the man said.

Joan managed a faint nod.

She readied herself to scream out.

His hand drew tight over her mouth for a second, and then it moved away.

Joan breathed in deeply . . . but she couldn't bring herself to scream.

She simply didn't have the energy.

As if this man had done something to stop her screaming out—had somehow manipulated an invisible hand to clutch her throat—she glared at him.

"Look, Mrs Albermonz—"

"Please stop calling me that," she said. "I left him last night."

The man didn't seem surprised to hear this information and this only served to raise Joan's suspicions.

But Joan told herself to stay calm, to wait for the right moment, to see what this man wanted. "Call me Joan," she said.

The man gave her the glimmer of a smile, and then he said, "Joan, I'd like you to listen to me very carefully, okay?"

Joan held still. She looked beyond the man to the door. If she ran for it right now, she might be able to make it out, be able to stick her head out there and raise the alarm.

The man looked about the penthouse, apparently *intimidated* for a moment or so. "Can I . . ." he trailed off as he looked about the place, his gaze finally falling on the little table and chairs set over by one of the French windows.

Joan paused for several moments and then she nodded.

The man smiled again, this time more widely. "Thank you," he said, and then took a seat on one of the chairs, keeping from sitting on the tail of his jacket with a flick.

Joan didn't sit.

She stood over him.

Her heart pounded.

Everything within her spelled out danger.

Told her to get herself shot of this man just as soon as she possibly could.

And yet there was also curiosity.

She wanted to know just what this man had in store.

"Who are you?" she said.

"I'm Mr Albermonz's accountant."

3

T HE MAN, who turned out to be called, Gregory Dawson—
or 'just Greg'—headed to the door of the penthouse and
returned with a briefcase.

Within the briefcase, he had a whole bunch of paper.

The whole thing was *filled* with paper!

Joan tried her best to keep her eyes on the man, to work out
whether or not he was going to give himself away somehow. If he
was going to show that he was out to cause *her* some harm.

The man . . . *Greg* . . . spent a good few minutes just shuffling
papers back and forth into neat, and not so neat, little piles. Joan
could've sworn that he shuffled every paper twice, from one side
to the other, till they were pretty much as they had been before.

As she scanned the information on the paper, reading it upside
down, she took in the many accounts all scrawled out there, all the
black smudges, the commas, the never-ending figures. It was
funny to think about how much of one person's wealth was intangible, existing only in the abstract. Only as numbers and commas
and decimal points.

When Greg had got through with whatever it was that he was
doing, the papers apparently now in the order which he wanted
from them, he glanced up at her and said, "Albermonz—your
husband—is having an affair with my wife."

Joan felt like she'd just been punched in the solar plexus. It was
impossible for her to take in. She hadn't thought, not for a second,
that her husband Richard might've been having an affair. He had
left no clues, no giveaway *smells*, nothing like that.

They had always shared a bed, right up until last night when
she had left.

She thought harder, tried to work out just where she might've missed some giveaway piece of evidence but, and maybe she was in shock, she could think of none.

Her mind turned back to Greg, sat before her, and she thought about how he must be feeling right at this moment. "I'm sorry," she said.

Greg gave her a hardy grin which disappeared seconds after it came into being. "It's okay," he said. "These things happen, however"—he met her eyes all of a sudden, his look intense, searching —"the time for feeling sorry for myself is gone, what I want now is revenge."

" 'Revenge' ?" Joan said.

Greg gave a nod and then returned to the pages all spread out before him. He flipped through a couple of them, and then, apparently reaching what he was looking for, slid one of the pages out. He slapped it down on top of the desk, and then tapped a figure in the centre of the page.

Joan read the figure, but it meant nothing at all to her.

Just some strange, exotic-sounding name along with a string of figures too long for her to even contemplate spelling out, even in her head.

She looked at Greg with a blank expression.

Greg kept his lips pert, tight, just totally under control. "Tax avoidance," he said.

"What?" Joan said, feeling like a real ditz.

"A refuge, an off-shore *scheme*, so that your hubby can get away without having to part with his cool, hard cash. Not really."

Joan looked again, down at the page. She read the name of the company:

Tario Investments.

She had come across that name before. She thought it through. Yes, that was it, back in the early days of her marriage she had come across it: a letter? Yes, she'd opened a letter by mistake. She had read the addressee as being to herself, the Mr Albermonz as Mrs.

Maybe there *had* been an extra 's' on the end, maybe it had just been a typo.

She remembered looking at the figure, seeing how long it was, and then she'd carried the opened letter up to Richard's home office. She did recall now how furious he had looked—just a flash, the first real time that she'd seen him angry . . . though she'd seen him angry plenty of times after.

He had almost snatched the letter from her, but Joan, still feeling innocent about the whole thing, about all of Richard's business, had found herself asking him what it was about. And Richard had told her something about a chain of factories he owned abroad.

Joan told this to Greg now.

Greg gave her another one of those brief smiles. "Nobody thinks about factories," he said. "At least, I've never come across an investor like Mr Albermonz *serious* about putting money into factories."

Yes, Joan was fairly sure that she'd known that.

. . . Or maybe she *liked* to think that she'd known that.

She turned her mind back to the present, met Greg's stare across the table. "And what're we going to do now?"

When Greg spoke again, there was no smile on his lips, and there was a deadness to his tone of voice. "We're going to ruin him."

4

ONCE GREG had done the necessary shuffling required, Joan found herself whisked along on this whole adventure. They got themselves out of the hotel, through a back door—apparently the same way that Grey had come in—and then they took a train for an hour to a city which Joan had never visited.

There, they checked into another hotel where Greg left her behind and went about his business. Joan could feel herself spinning around. It was almost enough to make her physically sick. What they were doing—what they were *about* to do—she just couldn't quite bring herself to believe it.

Over the course of their marriage, she had built up Richard as being this supernatural being, far too large for her, or anybody else for that matter, to take down.

And yet, here was this pokey little accountant about to bring Richard's whole empire tumbling to the ground.

She had pushed Greg as to just what her involvement was supposed to be, and he had hinted that her signature could be key to the whole matter.

But Joan couldn't quite sit easy with herself thinking about it.

In fact, she felt terribly uncomfortable about the whole deal.

About what they were doing.

Oh, sure, she and Richard had grown apart—they were *getting* a divorce—but did she really want to leave him in the gutter? Did she hate him so badly that she wanted to watch absolutely everything that he'd ever built in his life crumble to ash?

She wasn't so sure.

And as she sat about the hotel room, Joan felt even greater unease at the whole thing. She thought about how she had felt at the beginning of her relationship with Richard, how they had lived with that powerful—too powerful to last, apparently—*lust*.

Now it had come to this.

Petty little power games.

That was what it boiled down to.

Another question which lingered on Joan's mind was just what Greg had in mind for her after all this was done with. Already he had shown himself to be the vindictive sort of guy who would go to great lengths to severely damage someone's life under the guise of revenge, so how far would that revenge extend?

Did he see the snatching of Richard's ex-wife as being fair recompense?

Or did he just fancy a little romantic fling to take his mind off his unfaithful wife?

Whichever it was, Joan decided, right here, and right now, that she would simply have no part in it whatsoever. She was tired of just floating along at whichever man's whim.

She padded over to the cheap beige plastic phone which sat beside her bed, and, fingers trembling uncontrollably, she dialled out the familiar number of Squoremyre Hall.

5

THE PHONE CALL was done with in under a minute.

Richard was curt, but not impolite.

He thanked her for what she'd done, and he even went so far as to wish her well.

Though Joan would've liked to have said no when he'd informed her that he had left her account unblocked to tide her over in the meantime, she found that she couldn't.

To do so would mean her being homeless *and* penniless.

It wasn't easy for her to make a clean break from dependence so easily.

The way it played out in the end, it was just like a film.

She was propped up in bed, reading a book she had picked up out of the hotel reception, that was when she heard the sirens. Next thing she knew, her phone was ringing. Greg calling her from his own room. No doubt telling her that they needed to scram. A little after that, the ringing telephone was replaced by frantic, hammering knocks on her door.

Those continued until firm-voiced policemen arrived to take Greg away.

Joan heard Greg screaming out for them to take her too, that Joan was just as implicated in the whole thing as he was, but they paid him no attention.

Joan could never truly say that Richard didn't take care of her.

He knew how to dot the *i*'s and cross the *t*'s.

And as Joan lay there, on her frumpy, budget-hotel bed, she couldn't help smiling, planning out her new life. Away from Richard.

Free from guilt.

ANOTHER MONTH,
ANOTHER DEATH

1

THE LILACS BLOCKED Ferguson's sinuses in a heartbeat. It was remarkable, really, how such a beautiful flower could possess such deadly powers of nasal congestion. He wished that he could smell something other than that odourless scent of himself.

Something other than the tasteless *taste* of himself.

The organ music, at least, passed through him in mournful waves. The blackness which surrounded him—the ties and suits, and dresses—they all presented themselves to him with some sort of quiet beauty.

Though Ferguson had told himself many times over, *before* the time he had reached seventy years of age, that he wouldn't find himself caught in the whirl of the funeral circuit—forced along in its tow, whipped along to pay his last respects to this cousin, or that friend, or that acquaintance—*right over there*—he had failed to hold himself to it.

He had told himself lots of things, though.

Had made himself more promises than he could *ever* possibly hope to keep.

And, he supposed, in retrospect, this was just another one that he would never quite be able to stick to.

The granite walls of the church seemed to carry their own innate chill and it didn't seem to matter that there was a whole host of electric heaters generously scattered about the place. They only seemed to provide little pockets of heat on this brisk December day.

But Ferguson, standing as he did over one of those heaters, was determined to make the most of it.

He rubbed his hands together and shot a glance off in the

direction of the coffin, up there, on its stand, and his gaze drifted onto the silver-framed photograph perched on top.

He stared into her face, into her blue eyes.

Barbara.

His neighbour.

That was who she'd been.

He recalled the day when she'd moved into the bungalow beside him. How she'd strutted up the garden path, wearing what had seemed to him, even at the time, extremely *impractical* heels. And that floaty summer dress of hers, the same colour to match her eyes.

Her trio of grandchildren had traipsed after her like a whole host of child servants, each of them carrying out of the boot of her Volkswagen Beetle a suitcase—some piece of elaborate, embroidered luggage, and, without a doubt, a beaming grin.

They liked to spend time with their granny, Ferguson could see that right away. And as he'd stood there, curtain twitching at his window, dressed in his V-necked, bobbly jumper, he'd wondered whether she might've been some sort of a grand widow, whether she might've once lived the high life and was still reluctant to let it go.

Though Ferguson had never really thought of himself as being a perceptive individual, he had to give himself something of a break in this case, seeing as he had pretty much nailed his observation right away.

He recalled, as he'd stood about the whole afternoon of Barbara's arrival, and how he'd thought about how he was going to make his approach. He had chided himself, over and over, that he should be simply *neighbourly* . . . shouldn't have anything else at all.

That was the way that he would *get to know her* just a little better.

And, in any case, was there really anything other than friendship he wanted to offer?

... Well, there might've been a *little* more.

When Ferguson blinked another couple of times, the floaty organ music came back at him all at once. It brought his skin out in a whole series of little pimples. He felt somebody touch him on the elbow and, when he looked, he saw that it was Barbara's daughter: Jennifer.

Jennifer had those same blue eyes that her mother had had, but she had none of the figure, none of that bone structure, none of those high cheekbones. Jennifer had more *doughy* features. One of those faces which suggested, to Ferguson, that she'd spent far too much of her life chasing after children, rather than, like her mother, indulging herself in just about every luxury—known and unknown—on the face of the Earth.

"Thanks for coming," Jennifer said.

Ferguson just bowed his head. He laid his tongue down into the base of his mouth, still tasting that taste which was somewhere between blood and *nothing* . . . and which he knew was his own taste. He risked a deep breath in, taking in that putrid stench of lilacs once more. And then he shifted his head backwards, glanced up in the direction of the middle-aged man playing at the organ—the unmarried vicar's son.

"Would you like to sit with us?" Jennifer said, indicating the front row of the pews.

Ferguson followed her gesture, looked to the shoulders all nestled into suits or shielded with sable scarfs. He felt a slight glowing within himself, but he knew what his answer must be. With a slight shake of his head, and a gentle smile to Jennifer, he slipped off to one of the pews at the back, and sat himself right in the corner, in a place where, he knew, nobody needed to look at him.

2

THAT AFTERNOON, the afternoon of Barbara's arrival, Ferguson recalled that he'd been making himself a cup of tea. It was then that his Parkinson's had struck. It was always worse in the afternoons when he didn't take his medicine. But he hated the way that it tasted, that bitter, chemical taste on his tongue. And he hated the way that it made his mind groggy, how it seemed to block up the thoughts that would normally come tumbling through him at a million miles an hour—even at seventy years of age.

Ferguson had dropped the spoon he had been using to stir in the brown sugar his GP had forbidden him. The spoon had slipped out of his shaking hands, and landed on the floor, tinkling away at his feet as it found its new sense of equilibrium in the world.

He had just stared at the overturned spoon for a long time, inspecting his concave reflection obscured by the steel grain.

It was only when he'd stooped to pick it up that he'd heard the steady *clack-clack* of high heels tapping their way along the concrete slabs which made up his garden path.

He had cocked his head, in the direction of his front door, anticipated the bell.

Heard the first electronic *fizzle* of the poorly connected wires.

When he had opened the front door, she had been there, of course.

Staring right back at him.

Not exactly smiling, but not *frowning* either.

"Hello," Barbara had said, quickly, seeming like she wanted to get the greeting out of the way. "The lights won't come on in my house, and I was wondering if you might know something about the electrics here"—she wrinkled her nose—"seeing as your domicile appears to be a carbon copy of my own."

For a couple of seconds, Ferguson had remained in something of a daze. He had had to blink several times to break himself out of it. And, as he breathed in her strongly scented perfume—which had carried a slight zest of orange peels along with something he couldn't put his finger on—he noticed how he'd ceased trembling. That the shakes which'd seemed to have taken hold of him so relentlessly only moments ago had drifted away.

He had gone over to her house, had had to turn on his side to navigate her front hall which was completely stuffed full with her possessions.

Just like she'd said, there was no light anywhere.

It seemed like there'd been a power cut.

But Ferguson had power just like normal.

Though Ferguson knew next to nothing about electricity, how all these systems worked, he had twigged, after years of living alone and not wanting to call on the luxury that was an electrician, that often his best option was a little trouble-shooting of his own.

So he sought out the fuse box, which, just as Barbara had alluded to, was located in the same place as it was in his house—at the back of one of the kitchen cupboards. And it was there that he found the problem. One of the switches had been triggered. He read Barbara off the label stuck beside the trigger, told her that it was something in the bedroom.

It was then that Barbara thrust her finger up in the air, parted her lips slightly in just such a way that sent a shiver to the base of Ferguson's gut. And, just like that, she whisked right out of the kitchen.

After that, after Barbara had unplugged the hair-curling apparatus that'd tripped the switch, and Ferguson had flipped the power back on, everything was a blur.

Somehow, Ferguson had found himself back in his own house, having been flapped out of Barbara's with great rapidity. He had even tried to push his luck in inviting her around for a *neighbourly* cup of tea, and her brush-off had been so subtle that Ferguson could hardly even remember just how she'd done it.

Then again, he supposed that somebody like her—somebody like Barbara—had had a lifetime of practice at the art of the brush-off.

3

THE VICAR—a woman in her mid-sixties, and with a lardy gut which set her robe billowing—read her way through the service up at the parapet.

The words didn't matter to Ferguson, they simply drifted in through his ear, bounced about the confines of his skull a little while, and then they disintegrated into nothing.

He hadn't come here today for the *words*, after all.

He had come here for the memories.

As he felt himself falling deeper into a trance, losing himself to the vicar's drawl, which even seemed to neutralise the sharp scent of the lilacs, he felt somebody take a seat beside him on the pew.

He slipped a subtle sidelong glance.

Saw that it was Geoff.

Or *Digger* as everybody called him for some long-forgotten reason.

Ferguson regarded Digger, almost seven-feet tall, and skinny as a beanpole save for the little pot belly that looped out from his midriff. Today, just like everybody else, he wore a smart, black suit. A *funeral* suit. And Ferguson couldn't help thinking that Barbara would've been pleased to see how elegantly he'd turned out for today.

Barbara had *always* been about elegance.

4

I T WAS A RAINY AFTERNOON in March—one of those days where the sun never seems to fully rise, where the day almost seems to remain half done. As Ferguson sat on his favourite armchair—not for any reason other than it being insanely comfortable—he stared out into the gloomy afternoon, stared at the rain streaking its way down the pane of glass.

A snap of fingers brought him around.

He glanced over the small table that stood between himself and Digger, and then he turned his attention downwards, to the chess pieces there. The board was beaten up, it had probably once had black-and-white squares, but the blacks were now more like sun-faded purples, while the whites looked closer to jaundice yellows.

Just like always, Digger was toying with him, that way that really good chess players do. Ferguson often wondered why Digger ever bothered raising the idea of them playing chess. Digger always—without exception—won. The challenge for Digger, Ferguson supposed, had more to do with trying to make it *look* like a close game each time.

Ferguson glanced over the pieces, and then made the fatal move.

With a wily grin, Digger swept down, knocking over Ferguson's king with his bishop.

"Checkmate," Digger said, slumping back in his own armchair.

Ferguson continued to stare out the window, into the gloom. The streetlights were just blinking on now, and a yellowy-orange glow shed itself over the garden. It was then that Ferguson was certain he saw an apparition, something which, if he'd said it out loud, he was certain would land him in the nuthouse. So he stayed quiet for the couple of moments it would take for it to be real enough.

"Dig?" Ferguson said, still staring out the window. "You see that?"

"See what, pal?" Digger replied.

"That . . ." but Ferguson trailed off.

He didn't trust anybody these days, not even his *de facto* best friend. He was almost certain that everybody—the whole *world*—ganged up against him in an attempt to toss him, unceremoniously, from his autonomy. To turf him out of his home.

Digger got up out of his chair and he pressed his forehead to the glass, peered out into the ever-more gloomy afternoon. He stood there for a long time, and then, when he peeled back from the glass, he wore a confused expression. And then, slowly, so gradually that Ferguson felt the prickle of anticipation passing through his veins, Digger opened his lips.

"There a woman out there gardening?"

"Glad I'm not going crazy," Ferguson replied, getting up from his armchair. "You think we should go out and see what's what?"

"Guess we'd better," Digger said.

The two of them donned rain slicks: a pair of which Ferguson kept at all times hung up by the door. One of the rain slicks had once belonged to his wife. He'd come across it one day, but since she'd long ago passed away, and adding in the fact that rain slicks were just about as gender-neutral—and any other sort of neutral you could want—that it would be a waste to simply throw it away. Still, Ferguson made sure that he took *her* rain slick, handing over his own to Digger.

Ferguson led the way over the concrete slabs, and they passed across his lawn, stepped over the invisible line which marked the boundary between his property and his neighbour's. And there, sure enough, was Barbara: herself wearing a rain cape, with a sunhat on beneath the hood, on her knees, and planting flowers.

"Barbara?" Ferguson said.

Barbara turned, craned her neck upwards, startled. She held a trowel in her hand, and as she took in both Ferguson and Digger, she held the trowel to her chest as if simply seeing them there had been a strain on her heart. "Goodness," she said. "You scared the life out of me."

"What're you doing, Barbara?" Ferguson said.

Barbara seemed to consider this for a couple of beats. Her gaze left his, and then drifted down to the trowel she held snug in her hand. Then she said, "I was just planting the petunias—didn't want to miss the season." She glanced about herself with a steady smile. "I mean, it's not like I was going to let a little rain ruin it."

Ferguson held still. He really wanted to slip Digger a sidelong glance, but, at the same time, he knew that doing so would make their presence here seem more threatening still to Barbara. And he didn't want to be a threatening presence. He wanted to be her friend.

In the end, it was Barbara who broke the silence. This time she didn't make eye contact. "Look," she said, "I know how this must look—crazy old lady out in the rain tending to her plants—but I assure you that that's simply *not* what's going on here."

Ferguson couldn't help thinking to himself that she'd described just what it looked like to him in perfect terms. And most likely Digger felt the same too.

"All I ask," Barbara continued, "is to be left alone."

Ferguson felt his chest tighten.

This time Barbara did meet Ferguson's gaze. "Is that too much to ask?"

MUSIC FROM THE ORGAN played out again, and it drew Ferguson in with its swill. Though Ferguson must've sat through almost a hundred funerals in the course of his life—most of those happening towards his later years—he could never once make the connection between the human and the service itself. Almost like the best they could do here, in this church, was to summon ghosts, to bring out the phantom memories of a person.

Could a person ever really be summed up in a forty-five-minute-long service?

From Ferguson's experience, he couldn't say.

Ferguson felt Digger's straight-as-an-arrow posture beside him, and he resisted the urge to glance to his side, because he knew that he would, most likely, look angry. And Ferguson knew that he had no reason to feel angry. Not with Digger, anyway. Digger was just about the closest thing he had to family now—everybody else had deserted him, been all caught up in the tornado of youth . . . left him behind in the dust and dirt to be pecked at by the crows.

Ferguson looked to Barbara's family, all sat there, on the front row of the pews. He felt his stomach sink a little as he regarded the backs of their heads, the way that they all held their heads at that same slight angle, looking up to the parapet, to the vicar up there, warbling along, leading the singing.

He could see no tears streaking the faces of the family seated on the pews—no sign of emotion aside from shock, or, perhaps— thinking the matter through with a little more brutality—*indifference.*

What was it they said about how when people got old it was

like eternity was opening up around them—like the whole world was so irrevocably changed that dying was a mercy?

That was what they said, wasn't it?

With nobody around 'your age' weren't you always damned to simply be a stranger in a strange land?

But Ferguson didn't want to die.

He didn't see dying as a mercy.

He saw it as surrender.

And he had never run from a battle.

Not in his whole life.

6

THE SUMMER was a long and hot one, and, with Digger at his side—each of them with a glass of cool ale in their hands —they soaked up the rays in Ferguson's back garden.

It was a wonderful feeling, and the best part of it all was the way that feeling the sun on his bare chest reminded Ferguson of being much younger. He recalled how, back when he'd been a teenager and had worked at a bakery, how he'd cycle back home across a cross-country path, over the crushed long grasses. And how he'd stare into those bluish-grey waters and see his reflection there.

He could almost breathe in that grassy smell now, that odour of fresh earth, still tasting the freshly baked roll he had pilfered from the bakery and was now chewing on as he cycled beside the river.

Sitting out here, in the garden, it was almost as if he could still feel the uneven ground passing beneath his bike tyres, could still hear the *tick-tick* of his spokes as his wheels rotated.

He snapped back to the present, felt like there was somebody watching him.

When he glanced up, he saw that it was Barbara, looking over his freshly varnished garden fence. "You know," she said, "a woman could get an awful shock from such a sight."

Ferguson and Digger had both laughed at that, and Ferguson had noticed the smile on Barbara's mouth—it must've been a miracle . . . he had hardly ever seen her show off any sort of emotion ever since she moved in next door, let alone *smile*.

"Fancy a glass?" Digger said, his voice large, and merry, just like always.

Ferguson remembered watching Barbara's wide smile slipping gradually off her lips, to be replaced by a deadness in her eyes, as she seemed to stare through something—the 'mists' of time?—and become fixated.

"Not gone crazy on us?" Digger had said, apparently noticing this.

It was then that Ferguson had felt that unpleasant stirring sensation at the bottom of his gut and he'd known—*instinctively*—that something was wrong. That something wasn't quite right with Barbara. But, just like he always did when he felt that *snap* of intuition, he ignored it. But soon after Digger started into another of his hilarious army anecdotes, and that moment was soon forgotten to an alcoholic haze.

How Ferguson wished he had gone to check.

Had put on a shirt, rung that doorbell, and asked her if everything was all right.

But he hadn't.

How was *he* to know?

In the end, he didn't find out till, sat in his front room, the TV blaring this or that, he caught that flicker of red-and-blue lights passing about the periphery of his curtain. It wasn't an entirely unfamiliar sight, given the fact that everybody on his street was an old fogey—there were calls out here most days. Sometimes he never got himself up to go and curtain twitch.

But that day he *did*.

And as he stood there, staring out through the pane of glass, he watched the paramedics pad their way up to Barbara's front door —listened to the *thuds* as they first knocked, and then broke it down. Smashed it off its hinges.

Ferguson had never felt so powerless—so *impotent*—in his entire life. He had simply stood and watched, and waited. He wondered, in retrospect, why he didn't so much as leave his house, go out there and ask the paramedics.

But, he supposed, there had really been no point to it.

Even so, he could've stood up there, on his front doorstep, and asked them how it had happened.

He had found out soon enough, though.

Suicide.

A whole fistful of pills was what had done it.

Ferguson had wondered for so long, for so many weeks, whether he might've been able to prevent it in some way, if there was something he might've been able to say to make her change her mind. To show her that there was still a life worth living in this world.

But no.

7

A S THE SERVICE drew to a close with a prayer, Ferguson found his lips moving almost of their own accord, almost like he was lip-syncing to a song on the radio. He kept on facing forwards, looking to *her* coffin—and to the photograph of Barbara perched on top. Her coffin seemed to be a sort of a pinewood shade, and he couldn't quite square it with himself, decide whether or not that was what Barbara would've wanted.

Would she have wanted more pomp?

An oak casket with *tasteful* golden swirls along the side?

Who really knew?

After all, Ferguson had only been a neighbour, and she had always kept him at an arm's length. She had never allowed him to get close.

On the way out, Barbara's family all stood up at the door to the church, seeing the mourners off. Ferguson felt like he was in line to be taken up to the gallows, shuffling along with the rest of them. He could almost feel the creeping death on his heels, readying to take him. Was that what Barbara could no longer stand? The spectre of death hanging over her? Had it been too much for her to take, and had she wanted to remove one last thing from death's hands?

He could only speculate.

Ahead of him, Digger strode up, strong and proud, to Barbara's daughter, Jennifer, and he gave her a two-handed handshake. Jennifer remained dead-eyed, that same expression which Ferguson had read on Barbara's face on the day of her death—on that day they had invited her around to Ferguson's garden, to live again.

If only a little.

Perhaps that was what she could not take any longer.

Starting again.

For all Ferguson knew, Barbara had had enough of starting again to last her a lifetime.

And why would she want to make friends with a pair of geriatrics anyway?

As Ferguson readied to shake Jennifer's hand, he felt nothing but numbness—without and within—and he couldn't help thinking, clearly and succinctly to himself:

Just another month.

Another death.

BLEEDING HEARTS CLUB

JEAN HADN'T BEEN AT ALL CONVINCED when her best friend, Emily, had dragged her along to the *Bleeding Hearts Club*. She had thought that it sounded like one of those ghastly places where everybody sat about in a circle of plastic chairs, in some afterhours school hall and blubbered their way through a fistful of tissues.

Talking about their *feelings*.

But, Jean had to admit, she had been somewhat surprised when, with Emily dragging her forwards, they had entered this swish-looking office block, and settled into what—for want of a better word—was an *executive* meeting room: complete with plush, black leather, reclining chairs; and a *plusher* fine-oak table.

Jean had immediately felt that the peach, V-necked top with mud stains from gardening, and the seven-year-old black jeans she had gone with might be somewhat inappropriate. And perhaps she would've felt that if it hadn't been for her friend, Emily, dressing down in the same way, and wearing a hooded sweatshirt to boot.

When Jean took her place in one of the chairs, she almost felt herself sinking right away into the leather, and she had to pinch herself a couple of times as she waited for the rest of the group to filter in so that she wouldn't drift off to sleep.

She'd put in a long shift at the café today, and she would be heading out, in about two or three hours, to her night job at the bar on the corner of the street where she lived.

Although Jean saw the woman all passing in through the doorway in similar clothing choices to herself and Emily, she couldn't help—*almost subconsciously*—rubbing at the particularly large mud stain near the hem of her top with a little spit.

It wouldn't come out.

So she gave up.

Just seeing the stain, she reflected, reminded her of *him* . . . and how *he* would make those snide little remarks about the impromptu garden she had sprouted to life within the unseemly, dead little concrete courtyard out the back of her flat.

He could *say* whatever he wanted now.

Now she was done with him.

Once the meeting hall was near filled, a large-framed, blond-haired lady with a shapeless jumper got up and brought the door shut.

Jean eyed her all the way back down into her seat, and she felt a nudge in her side from Emily—sat next to her.

"That's Rachel," Emily whispered. "In charge of the group."

Jean just gave a slight nod as she kept her gaze on Rachel, observed how she produced a pair of thick-framed, plastic glasses from within the breast pocket of the blouse she wore beneath her jumper.

A silence drifted down over the room.

And something about the silence was unsettling to Jean.

But she tried not to give anything away.

Rachel glanced up from the notebook she propped open on the table, and finally—*inevitably*—her eyes came to rest on Jean. She smiled slightly, the wrinkles from the effort working their way up her cheeks and to the side of her face. "So," she said, "it looks like we have a new member."

"Uh," Jean immediately broke in, "I don't think *member's* really the right . . ." but her words were cut off due to a sharp prod in the ribs from Emily's elbow.

Rachel just smiled on, glanced back down at the notebook before her.

In that short time, Jean got a quick look about the meeting room. Took in all the faces of the other women all assembled here.

All of them with their private, emotional trauma. Jean wondered if they'd gone through something similar to her.

She felt a slight tightness in her chest.

Wasn't that the reason Jean had come?

Wasn't that the reason that Jean had *allowed* Emily to finagle her into joining her?

To *share.*

Rachel's eyes moved onto Jean's. "So," Rachel continued, "it's standard for new arrivals to tell us a little bit about themselves and the problems they're facing."

Jean held herself still.

This was silly—*so silly*—and yet she felt that little voice at the back of her mind.

The one which told her that she *did* need help.

Good thing she knew just how to silence *that* voice.

Jean looked about the room, feeling the weight of expectation on her. She drew in a deep breath. Pressed her lips together. And managed a shake of her head. "Nope," Jean said. "I'm doing just fine, actually."

Rachel continued to smile, but tilted her head slightly to one side. "Really?" she said, clearly not believing Jean.

"Uh huh," Jean said, slipping Emily a sidelong glance. "Just fine."

Rachel glanced about the other women in the room, and then, for a fraction of a second, down to the notepad before her. She clasped her hands together, and peered over the steeple she had created with her knuckles. "I think, Jean, that you need us far more than you believe. If you'll only . . ."

And it was then that Jean felt something within her snap. All the rage which'd been balling itself up at the base of her diaphragm seemed to just come busting on out. Before she knew it, she was on her feet. Headed for the door. She felt *their* eyes on her. *All* of them.

It *itched*.

This attention *itched*.

She needed to get . . . get *away*.

Jean fumbled the handle of the meeting room door a couple of times, but she got it open in the end, and before she really caught onto what she was doing, she was far along the hall.

The tears rolled down her face, the tears she had promised herself—*promised*—never to allow to take control again. But here they were. Back again.

She spotted the sign for the toilets, and she ventured towards them.

The soles of her battered old trainers creaked against the recently washed floor.

She slipped into the toilet, found herself immediately basking in beige lighting, in bronze basins, and in the slightly grey-purple shades of polished granite.

She thought about slipping into a cubicle, but considered it— even in her fragile emotional state—as a little too cliché, and so, instead, she took up her spot at one of the basins. She stared herself in the eyes in the mirror. The tears still came. She ran the cold tap. Dabbed her wrists beneath it. Felt the blood cool as it rushed about her body.

She could hear her heart beating hard.

In her eardrums.

A steady march.

Thrump-thrump-thrump . . . on and on, never-ending.

And then, the tight ball, the one at the base of her diaphragm, seemed to subside. She felt the calmness returning. The torment of her thoughts leaving her. She could think clearly again. It'd been a shock, that was all. Just too much for her to take in at one time. And it was over and done with now. She had extricated herself from the situation.

All over . . . all of it . . . *done with.*

In the near distance, she heard the gentle approach of footsteps.

But it didn't stir Jean's mind.

She remained focussed on her mirror image confronting her.

She wouldn't turn away.

Couldn't turn away.

She had to confront this.

Had to confront this now.

Or it might consume her.

She understood . . . understood it all . . .

Emily's familiar voice came to her, bundling along through the door to the toilets. "Jean?" she said. "Jean, are you in there?"

Jean sniffed a couple of times. Then she replied that she was.

"We'll be waiting for you when you're ready," Emily said, and then, with another few footsteps, Jean listened to her friend retreating.

They were leaving her alone.

Allowing her to come to her own senses.

There was no pressure here.

Jean saw that now.

It would all be on her own time.

Her own time for healing.

And, as she dunked her hands into the cold water flowing out from the taps, she couldn't help but repeat to herself, over and over in her mind, that she had been waiting a long time for this.

And finally that wait was over.

NOTHING PERPETUAL

1

THE *SCRUNCH-SCRUNCH-SCRUNCH* of beans was almost unbearable as Zach Evermaster went at his daughter's beanbag with a pair of scissors.

God, how he *hated* the damn thing!

Ever since his daughter Tara had come home from university with the beanbag, had laid it down in his beautifully-repainted, newly-carpeted sitting room, he had been conspiring ways that he might be able to get shot of it for good.

And, considering his deeply passive-aggressive nature, this seemed the most sensible way to go about it.

Still, Zach did feel faintly ridiculous, having lain in the dark beside his wife Lorna earlier tonight, waiting for the sound of her heavy breathing, a sure-fire sign she was sleeping, before sneaking off in just his boxer shorts—how he always slept—to slip into the kitchen and get the scissors.

So that he might be here.

Kneeling down on the carpet.

Feeling the *rough* texture dig into his bare kneecaps.

As Zach scissored at the beanbag in the darkness of the sitting room—it was *important* that he work under cover of darkness—he could feel the sweat trickle down from his temples, and drool down the sides of his face. He could smell its salty odour. And a couple of those salty beads of water snuck in through his dry lips.

Once he'd got a decent tear opened in the beanbag—no larger than about a coin in size—he experimented.

He plumped up the bag and watched a fine trickle of beans slip through.

He smiled to himself.

Yes, that was better.

Much better.

It almost made him want to shake his head to think of it now. Of how his daughter had thought that bringing this fire-red monstrosity to bear on his beautifully-toned, lightly-coloured, lime-juice green colour scheme that he had spent literally *hours* trying to get right would be a welcome proposition.

And that was before Zach got to thinking about the *stains* on the beanbag.

The fact of the matter was that Zach had felt that he could no longer spend time in his own sitting room. That, whenever he sat down on the sofa to watch TV, or whenever he wanted to crack open a good, heavy book, that *bright-red* beanbag was always in his line of sight.

Something had had to give.

And he had done just what *needed* to be done tonight.

He should've been *proud* of his work.

So, as he straightened up, allowing the scissors to dangle down at his thigh, why did he feel somewhat numbed inside?

Why was it that he felt just a touch of sadness emanating from his gut, and threatening to swallow him whole?

For some reason, he couldn't shake the image of a mean old man coming along with a hatpin at a fairground and popping some unsuspecting child's balloon . . . not even pausing as he walked by to speculate on the theoretical child's tears.

But his daughter wouldn't *cry* about this, would she?

She wouldn't even *know* that there had been any malice involved.

Beanbags were beanbags.

Why, Zach imagined that, at any given minute, somewhere in the world, there was a beanbag getting punctured.

Fingernails.

Splinters on the floors.

High heels.

There was *no* question, something was *certainly* doing for these beanbags.

It was just that, in this case, there had been some conscious involvement in the demise of this particular beanbag.

Not that Zach was ashamed.

The beanbag had *had* to go.

Finished with his work, at least for now, Zach snuck out of the sitting room.

He pried himself back beneath the duvet, beside his wife Lorna's warm, sleeping body.

And, for the first time since his daughter had brought the beanbag home, he *smiled*.

2

THE NEXT DAY—*Saturday*—Zach woke up around half past nine. It was a good hour, or two, longer than he was accustomed to sleeping. Usually, during the week, he would get himself up around eight so that he would head off to *Dunesbury*; the accountancy firm where he worked. But not as an *accountant* . . . that was always a particularly annoying point to explain to people whenever he had to tell them that he worked *at* an accountants' . . . they almost *always* made that agonising leap to saying, "Ah, that must be dull," or words to that effect, and then Zach would have to set them straight.

Tell them that he was a standard-issue, IT grunt.

Why he didn't just say that he 'worked in IT' plainly whenever people asked what he did was one of the Great Mysteries of the World . . . certainly something never to be divined by him . . .

But today was certainly not a workday.

All the same, he supposed that the late hour of his waking had to do with the stress of the previous night. Had something to do with the sly task he had been carrying out under the mask of darkness.

He really wasn't getting any younger.

He could easily empathise with other fifty-something men who often claimed they 'didn't do' late nights any longer.

Zach glanced about the bedroom, saw that his wife Lorna was already gone. She had opened the window a crack and Zach could just about hear the birdsong floating in. Could hear the *hush* of the motorway not far off. Could breathe in the roses which were flourishing just outside the bedroom window.

Zach recalled his doubts when he and Lorna had been searching for a house—almost twenty-five years ago to the day.

Lorna had brought him along here to this suburban development, far from the City. It had struck Zach as odd, at first, that anybody would choose to live in an ex-field in the middle of nowhere. And yet, here they were.

Zach had grown up in a townhouse. It had been five storeys, and Zach had had the attic room. The smallest room. Being the youngest of three brothers, he supposed that was his lot: a sort of *burden* if he liked to think about it in piteous terms. He had arrived late to the Party of Life and he was negated all those privileges bestowed on his earlier-born siblings.

Bastards.

Still, it had been pretty good training for life itself.

That townhouse had seemed to be positioned right in the middle of everything—and *anything*—and still to this day, Zach sometimes woke up in the early hours of the morning and listened, somewhat stunned about the degree of silence—the *tranquillity*— that hung to this suburban development.

There were no slamming doors. No drunken, out-of-control voices. And absolutely no sounds of smashing glass as a bar fight got kicked out into the street.

And Zach wasn't sure whether or not he liked it.

Of course, back in the townhouse, back in his youth, all of those things had surely disturbed his beauty sleep, but it had also added a certain colour to his surroundings.

There was *always* something going on.

Although Zach didn't like to think about it too much, he wondered if his somewhat control-freak persona had leaped out at him as soon as he and Lorna had set down the first instalment for this, their *bungalow* home.

But, on mornings like this, on mornings when he understood the concept of 'smelling' victory, Zach really did appreciate the peace and quiet. Being able to peer out through his bedroom window and into his garden. Then out beyond, to the fields sprawling away from his house into the discernible distance.

All golden in the morning sunlight.

From off somewhere in the house, Zach heard glass smashing.

He straightened up immediately.

Heart beating hard.

A slight taste of the passable spinach lasagne Lorna had cooked last night at the back of his throat.

He reached about himself, propped himself up on his mattress, and then, feeling his pulse pounding hard at his temples, he pried himself right out of bed.

On his way out of his and Lorna's bedroom, he grasped hold of his fluffy, white dressing gown which hung off the back of the door, and brought it swooping about his shoulders. With a neat motion, he tightened the belt.

That was the thing about Company—and his daughter now qualified in *that* category—it meant he couldn't go wandering about the house in just his boxer shorts.

3

T HE KITCHEN SMELLED strongly of coffee, and when Zach glanced over in the direction of the counter, where the cafetiere always stood, he saw all that was remaining was a grungy, brown-black mulch. The cafetiere had capacity for three cups of coffee. His wife Lorna was an early-riser. Without exception, she got herself up and about the world at six o'clock on the dot. She would then go make a cafetiere of coffee. And, sometimes —on *special* occasions—she would bring Zach his first cup in bed.

Since Zach had to go out to work, he never got around to having that second cup of coffee, and since his wife Lorna stayed at home during the day, she most likely drunk the remainder of the cafetiere around midmorning.

Not that Zach had *ever* witnessed this event.

He prided himself on never having missed a day's work in his life.

And whenever he took holidays, he made a point of never wasting a whole day just loitering about the house.

That was somewhat beside the point, though. The fact of the matter was that Zach immediately saw that all three cups had been depleted. That despite the fact that there were only *three* of them in the house, one of the other two had seen fit to knock back a second cup of coffee. To say that Zach was severely displeased was an understatement.

But what came next put him in an *even worse* mood.

Zach glanced down at the kitchen floor, a flurry of activity, with his wife Lorna and his daughter Tara on their hands and knees, each of them with a dustpan and brush.

That was funny, Zach had never thought that they had *two* dustpans and brushes.

He supposed that he learned something new every day.

With a flick of her honey-shaded hair, Tara beamed up at him. "Sorry, Dad," she said, her chirpy morning voice perhaps a clue to the mystery of the missing second coffee . . . or, more drastic, a sign that she had inherited her mother's getting-up-early gene. "Did the noise wake you?"

Zach crunched his eyes shut, and then opened them again. He stared down at the scene. At the broken fragments of glass which twinkled in the sunlight pouring in through the window. "No," he said, not putting any of his heart into his reply.

Tara smiled back at him, and she resumed her brushing.

Zach turned his attention in the direction of Lorna—the mirror image of Tara, except that she had golden blond hair streaming down the back of her pink pyjamas. She concentrated hard on her brushing, not so much glancing up at Zach to wish him good morning, or anything.

She was all business.

As *always* in the mornings.

Although Zach tried not to allow it to rankle him, rankle him it *did* that his wife made four times what he did.

And *from home.*

Now, Zach was the last person he would consider to be a misogynist. Actually, he had always considered himself fairly liberal. There had never been any indication that—recently married, having just moved into the bungalow—Lorna had any sort of artistic ambition, let alone *talent.*

But, well, that just went to show how much she'd kept *hidden* from him.

When the two of them had got married, Zach had been working the job he was still working now . . . at an accountants' but not actually an accountant . . . and Lorna had been the secretary at the accountants'.

When they'd first started going out, Zach had felt like quite the playboy about the accountants' office. It was a well-known fact that just about all the men there had 'made a play' for Lorna and been rebuffed. And, still to this day, Zach wasn't certain what it was that had sprung him into action . . . maybe it had been the extra cup of coffee he'd had at breakfast that day, or the adrenalin that'd bolted through him when he'd bunged someone's fender with his own in the car park. Although Zach hadn't left any lasting damage to the fender, he had slipped a note beneath the windscreen wiper of the victim's car.

The point was that *something* had got him riled.

Pumped him up.

And he had asked her for a date.

Lorna had accepted.

Things had gone on just as Zach had planned once he'd got the engagement over and done with, the two of them continuing to work at the accountants' until they'd scraped together enough for a house deposit and a wedding.

It'd been about a year, all told.

Their connection had been somewhat superficial, just pretty much chatting about what they'd watched together on TV the night before, or where they should go away next for a weekend mini-break.

However, marriage all done with, house all bought and paid for —the first instalment of the *mortgage*, anyway—Lorna had one day, seemingly out of nowhere, asked if she could, maybe, have one room of the house for her 'studio'.

Although Zach'd been somewhat unsure about the phrasing, he hadn't challenged it, thinking that it might've been some sort of a fashionable way of speaking about a 'home office', or whatever. And since it was Lorna who did the household bookkeeping, it seemed only natural that she have a space to stick up some filing cabinets: a desk to push numbers around on.

So, imagine his surprise when she informed him that she would quite like to have the garage as her 'studio space'.

Again, Zach hadn't protested, and he hadn't really thought a thing about it any further—except that it was a *mite* odd—until this dirty great lorry had showed up outside the house one day, a man in overalls stepping off it with a clipboard grasped in his hands.

Standing on the doorstep, on a Saturday afternoon—as Zach recalled it—he had observed Lorna, beaming from ear to ear, trot up to the man with the clipboard and sign for everything he had there.

And Zach had watched on as Lorna and the man with the clipboard had worked together to shift a whole bunch of cloth-covered mysteries off the back of the lorry. Although Zach didn't find out about the *precise* contents until later . . . until he had straight-up asked Lorna about the delivery in the hope of some explanation . . . he could still recall the inventory of the order:

Easel.

Oil paints.

Wooden stool.

. . . And a whole lot else *besides*.

When—let alone *why*—his wife had decided that she'd wanted to become a painter really was one of those unfathomable mysteries. And it wasn't like he hadn't *tried* to speak with her about it.

For God's sake, whenever he would bring it up, ask her how her painting was going, she would, invariably, inform him that it was 'fine', clearly hinting, either by flat changing the subject, or by bustling off to do some suddenly *urgent* activity, that he should just drop the whole thing.

That Zach shouldn't even *attempt* to understand.

And so Zach *had* given up attempting to understand.

Truth be told, things had remained that way, with Zach not going *anywhere near* the topic for years, just accepting the evenings and weekends his wife spent in the garage without need for further explanation. Until one night when Lorna had gone out with friends.

That had been one of those rarest of nights, when Zach had decided to get himself down to helping out with some of that aforementioned household bookkeeping.

His specific focus *that* evening had been Tara's—then nine—university fund, because, it was an established fact, between Lorna and Zach, that Tara *would* be attending university.

As Zach had been glancing along the columns of numbers, the savings account balance, that he realised, even accounting for the odd bonus-related pay here; cashing in unused holiday time there; they would be well off the mark.

Not so much as a *quarter* of the way to having enough by the time that Tara turned eighteen.

While Zach had sat at the kitchen table, the gentle notes of a funk song drawling out of the quiet radio sitting up on the kitchen counter, he recalled the gentle *hum* of Lorna's car purring its way up into the drive. Then the slamming of the driver's door.

It was right then, and Zach, still to this day, really had no idea *quite* where it had come from, but he caught onto the idea that this would be one of those apocryphal moments.

A severe tingle down his spine.

The idea that something like a bowling ball was about to smash through the walls of their home, and utterly change everything.

Forever.

In all honesty, as Zach listened to the vaguely sad sounds of Lorna shucking her high heels out in the hall, jettisoning her coat over its peg with the *rustle* of fabric, he sincerely believed that Lorna had found someone else.

That she had come across someone else, in the course of her socialising with her friends, who was a better fit than Zach by factors of ten.

Zach had expected it for so long.

And Zach's fear—that slightly bloody taste in his mouth—had only increased when he'd set eyes on Lorna standing there in the doorway to the kitchen. Complexion pale. Her red lipstick only making her lack of colour more obvious. Trembling ever so slightly.

Zach had held his hands down by his sides, and dug his fingernails into his palms.

Felt the pain pinch at him.

Then Lorna had told him about the paintings.

About how she'd *sold* some of her paintings.

And for *how much*.

The phrase 'shell-shocked' sprung to Zach's mind, over and over again, whenever he reimagined the incident.

4

"THAT SHOULD BE IT," Tara said straightening up, the dustpan down at her side, and the glass fragments nestled safely within.

Lorna did the last of her brushing and then stood up beside their daughter.

Zach could feel his chest quite tight. And he was already beginning to get those shakes from not having immediately administered himself his daily dose of caffeine. When he met Lorna's eye, he managed to raise a smile. "What's been breaking this morning then?"

Lorna smiled back at him.

Not the smile of a *lover* . . . more like the smile of a fond, older, wiser sister . . . even though Zach was a good seven years her elder . . .

Lorna gave a shrug and turned her back to him, moving towards the large cardboard box where they left all the finished-with newspapers. "One of those silly things—you know, one of those things which we pick up over the years."

"What thing?" Zach said, suddenly curious.

From the way that Tara was staring at the side of Zach's face, Zach could tell that this was more than just a trinket that had *got* broken. And, more to the point, that Zach was supposed to be getting angry about it . . . even though Zach never got angry about *anything* . . . at least, he never *thought* that he got angry about anything . . .

Already, her back still turned to him, Lorna had made good progress on wrapping this broken thing with newspaper. She was now in the process of taping said broken thing up in its impromptu packaging.

The kitchen was awash with silence for a long while.

Zach decided that this was just one of those better-to-drop-it things. He glanced back at the cafetiere, gave a slight sigh, and then made inroads on washing it out.

"Oh," Tara said, "sorry, I can do that for you, Dad."

Without him so much as surrendering anything, Zach felt Tara's smooth, dainty fingers unravelling his grip from the cafetiere. Before Zach knew what was happening, Tara was turning the tap to full gush and was rinsing out the gunk from the cafetiere.

Steam rose up into the air.

It felt moist against Zach's cheeks. He could feel a sneeze coming on.

Maybe he'd get a cold.

That would be a *fine* way for him to start his weekend.

"Got up early this morning," Tara explained, as she washed out the cafetiere, "couldn't get back to sleep again, so thought I'd come and make some coffee."

So, that was the reason, the delicately balanced weekend ritual had been prodded off its scales. Sent tumbling to the ground with *smashing* force, just like had befallen the mystery glassware.

"You couldn't sleep, so you made coffee?" Zach said.

Tara shrugged—just like her mother did. "Yeah, not much point in trying to sleep, so thought I might have a go at staying awake."

Zach was rendered stunned as he observed Lorna carrying the bundled-up newspaper ball, containing the broken glass, off through the house.

Zach heard the front door creak open, and he listened to Lorna treading all the way out to the garage. He listened to her come all the way back in again, scrub her slippers on the doormat and then bring the door shut once more. When she passed back through the kitchen doorway, Zach squinted at her face, trying to make out something.

Anything.

But he couldn't.

She was as much of a puzzle to him as the day they'd met.

As the day they'd *married.*

As the day she'd announced she wanted to *paint.*

Without giving Zach any more of a chance to untangle her, though there was little chance of that with their marriage this far along, Lorna took up her place at the kitchen table. She sat down, pressed her shoulders against the chair back and sighed out.

Hard.

As if she'd just taken part in some sort of manual labour.

Artists, what a bunch of melodrama!

"Have a seat, Dad," Tara said, measuring out the ground coffee into the cafetiere, and allowing a large amount of it to sprinkle *all over* the kitchen counter, "you look like you could do with a strong one."

"Yes," Zach said, seeing the kitchen chairs and imagining some sort of an oasis.

When he sat down, he gave Lorna another of his pleasant smiles.

And she smiled *pleasantly* back.

Sometimes Zach wondered what Lorna thought about their relationship, about this arrangement of theirs which they—somewhat shabbily—called a *marriage.*

Did it come through in her art?

Would scholars, years down the track, heads tilted as they observed one of Lorna's paintings in a gallery, mumble something about 'sexual frustration' or 'noble silence in the face of disapproval', or a 'looming, silent, dark figure with a somewhat *negative* influence?'

No, he was probably just getting too far into it.

Why would Lorna waste her time thinking about *him?*

Still, it did frighten Zach *somewhat* to think that something along those lines might find its way into an art textbook, or whatever it was that art students learned from in the future.

A few minutes later, a short chat about the weather with Lorna and Tara over, Tara brought his coffee to him at the table. Laid it down before him. And Zach lost himself in the spiralling steam as it unfurled. He breathed in the slightly wicked, bitter odour of the coffee, already feeling himself salivating at the prospect.

Was this what they called addiction?

. . . Nah, addicts were those people who slept in gutters and sold their grandmother's silver for a hit . . . whereas Zach, well, he slept in a peaceful suburban neighbourhood, in a *bed*, no less, and the only thing which he sold was his soul at his day job.

Zach had got about halfway through his affair with his morning coffee when he noticed the silence pressing on at him from all sides. He glanced up over the rim of his cup, almost having forgotten that a world *did* exist beyond that scrap of porcelain.

Tara and Lorna both stared back at him.

"What?" Zach said, frowning slightly, then putting his cup down on the table. "What's the matter—why all the mystery about that broken *thing?*"

Tara and Lorna exchanged glances, and then Tara, apparently having been predefined to deliver the news, turned on her best puppy eyes and said, in a deeply—*truly*—regretful voice, "Dad, it's about that glass . . . about the one that work gave you, you know, to celebrate twenty years with them?"

All at once, Zach felt memories streaming through his brain. Almost like he was sat on a train. He watched all the colours blurring into one. All those rays of light which he had no chance at all

of grabbing a hold of. He could only see the snatches. The cere-
mony at work. How Zach had gone in *that* day knowing full well
just what that morning signified. That he had been at *Dunesbury*
for twenty years the second he'd stepped in through the door. He
thought about his daily routine. How he'd gone about the whole
morning without anybody saying anything. How he'd eaten lunch
alone. When Zach had returned from lunch, as always, five
minutes early to start work in the afternoon, he had decided to
take the afternoon off . . . so that he might spend some time alone .
. . perhaps go drive his car somewhere deep—*deep*—in the countryside . . . then leave the engine running . . . be alone with his
thoughts.

But as he'd walked back in through the front door of the office,
he had heard muffled voices, some sort of *electricity* in the air, and
that was an *extremely* easy thing to latch onto at *Dunesbury* seeing
as, for the most part, nothing ever happened.

There wasn't much to get excited about working at an
accountants'.

Not for the grunts, in any case.

It wasn't until Zach had taken several steps into the office, felt
the slippery soles of his work shoes make contact with the thread-
bare carpet, that Lorna had emerged from—*seemingly*—nowhere.

She had been wearing a wry smile.

And Zach had found himself catapulted back, to many years
before.

He had thought about the day he had asked her out. How he
had been trembling all over, either from the caffeine, or from the
nerves. Then he had wondered what she'd been doing there. He
knew that she no longer worked at the accountants'. That she had
quit the moment that her painting had taken off. And yet . . . and
yet . . . she had *been* there.

Lorna hadn't said anything at all, she had merely taken hold of his hand and led him along the corridor, into the back of the building where, in the main presentation room, there was a huge cake awaiting him. Multi-coloured party streamers hanging down from the roof. Everyone looking ridiculous in their work clothes, with pointed party hats held to their heads by cheap elastic bands.

Zach had thought that he'd taken a wrong turn.

Ended up in some parallel universe.

Or maybe he'd hit his head . . .

But it had been real, and, once the afternoon entertainment unfurled, his boss had presented him with a glass: one with a golden rim, and silver lettering with the name of the firm: *Dunesbury*, sketched onto it.

Just below the name of the firm had been, written out in a cursive font:

In celebration of 20 years' service.

And although Zach had always believed himself a long way from sentimental, he had to admit that, as he gave the speech which his colleagues barked out for in their tipsy states, he could feel a lump in his throat.

Someone cared.

Someone *did* care.

About *him*.

And about what he had done with his life.

5

ZACH FELT THE COLOURS unblur themselves, and the kitchen returning to him—*reality* returning to him. It was almost like he was being cut free.

Wake up and smell the coffee!

He *could* smell the coffee.

Still a good half cup to go.

Trembling as he reached for the cup, Zach speculated about those other thoughts which'd been going through his mind that day. The day when they celebrated his twenty years of service. How Zach had been intending to head into work, ask for the hours off in the afternoon, and to drive himself to a quiet spot . . . out in the countryside . . . and then . . . and then . . . well, who would've known?

Who would've *cared*?

When Zach knocked back the remainder of his coffee, he found that Lorna and Tara were still staring at him, the way a pair of bomb disposal experts might look at a bomb knowingly having made some fatal error. Just waiting for the *blast* to hit.

Zach felt the caffeine humming through him. He knew that he was still trembling.

Tara's voice cut through the silence. "I'm sorry, Dad," Tara said, genuine tenderness in her voice. "We thought . . . we thought that we should wait till you'd had your morning coffee before telling you. Mum said that you're much better at processing things once you've had your caffeine."

Though Zach understood every one of Tara's words, he couldn't quite bring his mind together enough so that he might be able to respond to them. Just . . . all this . . . everything seemed so *utterly* beyond his comprehension.

143

"Dad?" Tara said.

Zach turned his head in her direction.

"I'm really sorry.

As Zach regarded his daughter, he saw that her eyes were glassy with tears. That she expected punishment, just as she might have done when she'd been ten years younger.

Zach breathed in.

He breathed out.

Then he set his cup of coffee down on the kitchen table.

Taking extreme care with his movements, not wanting to show off his trembling too much if he could help it, he trod over to his daughter. She sat down below him, her head tilted up to him. A single tear ran down her cheek.

Zach smiled. He crouched down.

And embraced her.

Felt her warmth.

The—*at first*—stunned deadweight of her body.

Then he felt her arms around him.

At first they were loose, she seemed hardly able to make a grip.

And then she squeezed him tighter.

Much tighter.

Next thing Zach knew, he could feel the arms of his wife around him.

Between his shoulder blades.

It was a sensation almost like he was encapsulated by freshly tumble-dried laundry.

Somehow it was the happiest he had been for some time.

One of those moments which seemed to creep close to his ear, and whisper, "It's okay—keep going."

When the hug ran its course, Zach got himself up, laid his emptied cup in the sink and went into the sitting room. He picked up the book he'd left lying on the coffee table and slumped down, still in his dressing gown, on the sofa.

As he turned the pages, he couldn't help noticing the beanbag.

Still there.

Sitting right in his eye line.

Zach shook his head and smiled, unable to quite believe it.

He returned to his book.

Zach had got through about three pages when Tara sauntered into the room. She made a beeline for the beanbag, one of her university reading packs clutched beneath her arm: really just a jumble of copies all held together with one of those string clips.

Without missing a beat, she dropped down onto the beanbag.

It happened too fast for Zach to say anything.

And—*anyway*—what would he have said if he'd had the chance?

Zach gripped his book hard. He felt his heart lump in his throat. His blood ran cold as he speculated about the very worst which could happen.

He expected Beanageddon, of course he did, but he didn't want his daughter to get harmed in the process.

But as Tara made contact with the beanbag, she sank down into it.

There wasn't so much as a single bean spilled.

Tara flashed a smile at Zach and then peeled back the pages of her copies, apparently returning to the spot where she'd left off her reading.

Zach tried to turn his attention back to his own reading, but found that he simply couldn't concentrate. How *could* he concentrate now?

He shut his book with a *slap* of escaping air and stared at Tara. "You, uh," he began, not really sure how he was going to put this at all.

Tara bent her head up to him.

Eyes wide.

Lips slightly parted.

"It's just," Zach continued, "last night—I noticed that there were a few . . . *beans* scattered about the carpet, and, well, I thought that there might . . . there could be . . ."

"A tear?" Tara butted in, still smiling.

She shrugged as she returned to her reading.

"Nah, happens all the time," she said. "Just needs a bit of needle-work—that's all."

" 'A bit of needlework?' " Zach repeated.

Tara glanced back up at him. "Yeah," she said, and then hoiked herself up off the beanbag. She allowed her reading materials to drop into a crumpled heap. Next, she grabbed hold of the beanbag, turned it upside down and pointed to a spot which, Zach could see, had been sort of pinched together.

The spot which he had cut open the night before.

"See?" she said, and then dropped the beanbag back down, shaking her head. "You do realise that I'm not a complete hopeless case, you know?" She drew in a deep breath. Sighed it out, then added, "Sure, I might be a butter fingers, but it's not like they breed *all* the practicality out of us at uni." She glanced back up at him. "Remember when I went through *that* sewing phase?"

Zach was lost in his own little world for several moments.

Then he snapped himself back.

He blinked a few times, if only to remind himself of the reality before his nose.

"Oh, yes," Zach replied eventually.

Tara rolled her eyes and returned to her reading. "Dads," she said, shaking her head again. "Just no accounting for them."

As Zach sat there, on the squashy sofa, soaking up his failure to get shot of the beanbag from his sitting room, he couldn't help thinking that—*somehow*—things were better this way.

Maybe there were *other* ways for him to make his mark on the world.

Like, other ways than destroying his daughter's beanbag.

. . . Perhaps he could have his own studio.

WHEREAS

T HE SHOULDER PADS weighed heavy across the width of Alexandra's back. Today it had been so cold that she had simply grabbed for the warmest-looking coat which hung off the hat stand by the front door of her home. The coat had turned out to be her brother's, and it had this fuzzy, cat fur-like lining to it. Every time the material brushed up against Alexandra's skin, she felt a warm glow plough through her.

Get her right down to the bone.

She could still taste the bitter grounds of the takeaway coffee she had slugged back not five minutes ago. It had smelled burned to her, but she hadn't complained. She always bought her coffee from the same elderly woman in the marketplace. Whenever Alexandra walked through the marketplace, in the mornings, whenever she felt the woman's gaze pass over her, the previous day's experience was always forgotten. And she would buy from her again.

It was only a few quid.

Alexandra crunched along the icy cobblestones of the town. She could hear, a little way behind, the hustle and bustle of the retreating market. People buying, and selling. She tuned them all out, managed to channel into the smooth, twittering birdsong in the distance. The birds which clung onto the branches and somehow made themselves heard over all the ruckus of mankind.

She went around the corner and found herself standing before a man who sat—slumped-over—on an up-turned plastic bucket.

He held his face in his hands and stared through his fingers at the grey, *grey* ground.

Alexandra took in his profile. The way that he wore a brown leather coat, scuffed in places, and with holes here and there. A thick, fluffy, multi-coloured jumper poked through the gaps in the leather. He seemed lost in thought.

Lost in thought over the cobblestones.

When Alexandra drew closer, she realised he was mumbling to himself:

"The way some people think, it comes and goes in cycles,
One day it's there, and the next it's gone.

When a heart breaks open, cracks down on the pavement, there's blood everywhere,
Nobody can deny that.

"Whereas with animal desire—and pain—there's no in between,
It's just feeling.

Over and over, and over, and over, again,
Nobody thinks, they just do."

Apparently finished, the man glanced up at Alexandra. She saw that his eyes were webbed with bright, red veins, and that they had a real bulging quality to them, as if they were simply too substantial to remain within their sockets.

She screwed up her eyes and glanced at him akilter. She spotted the faded, navy-blue beret lying on the ground beside the man. Within, he had several coins—mostly coppers—and a pair of five-pound notes.

The man was still staring at her as if she had disturbed him in the most private of moments. He held himself so still that he reminded her of a deer which has run out from a woodland, right into the middle of the road, and stands stunned before the bright headlights of an approaching car.

Doomed.

"What is it?" Alexandra said.

The man continued to stare at her. He didn't reply.

"What you were saying—what you were mumbling?"

Again, no response.

Alexandra might as well not even have been there.

Not even have stood before him.

But she *was* standing before him.

She was *speaking* to him.

And she expected an answer.

"Excuse me?" she said, agreeing with herself that this would be the final time she attempted conversation before hoiking herself back off home.

The man remained silent.

Alexandra glanced back down at the beret, and she fished about in the pocket of her brother's coat. She produced a scattering of coins and she allowed them to tumble down through her fingers, to drop silently into the beret.

With a final look to the man, she continued on her way, along the side alley.

It was only when she was about to turn the corner, to leave the man behind, both in her mind-space as well as geography, that she heard his muffled voice once more.

Speaking to her.

His low, throaty drawl.

Alexandra didn't turn around. She just stood still.

Stared at the rugged, stone wall which sat right before her eyes:

"When nobody lives, nobody cries,
And when the house burns down who's around?
Fight they may, fight and fight and fight,
But whereas."

Alexandra felt her chest tighten a touch.

There was something—*something* about those words.

Something she couldn't quite wrap her head around.

But, as she thought to herself as she turned the corner, and left the man behind—the man she had never once seen lurking in this alley before—she would certainly bear those words in mind.

THE UNLIKELY BIBLES

1

TERRANCE HAD TO ADMIT, when he'd first seen the name *The Unlikely Bibles* in today's programme, he'd thought that he'd find himself facing off with some—*abhorrently hip*—band of musicians. Ones who thought their music escaped bar band-dom and stretched its wings into the realms of *theatre*.

But, then again, in this job, nothing was *ever* what he thought.

Terrance stretched himself out in the tanned-leather, well-worn in—and *ridiculously comfortable*—chair. It sent the coils creaking lightly. He breathed in its distinctive smell. Felt the *toughness* bite at the back of his throat. Breathing in the scent of the chair was almost like chewing into an extremely well-cooked steak.

Almost.

He glanced about him, to the other producers surrounding.

As always, as with *all* acts, the producers were all posed somewhere between instant, first-sight love—leaning eagerly forward in their chairs, their mouths ripped open in great big dirty grins—while others were slumped back, their fists propping up their unbearably *heavy* heads.

All the producers were dressed in sharp suits.

Shades of charcoal, sable and—as Terrance liked to think of his own suit—*the night.*

Terrance crossed his legs and stared at the jiggling toe of his polished black shoe for several moments. He observed the shine his shoe gave off from the sharp, too-bright theatre lights. Then, not wanting to appear rude—the same couldn't be said for other producers—he glanced back up at the act.

Comedy.

That was it.

Wasn't it?

His eyes sketched the stage, back and forth, though there wasn't all that much to take in.

The scenery was minimal.

Just the bare stage.

A pair of actors.

They *were* actors.

Weren't they?

Both the actors were dressed in beige trench coats which came down to their ankles.

One male:

Stark, *fearsome* jawline.

Buzz-cut blond hair.

One female:

Sad, light-blue eyes.

The same buzz-cut blond hair.

He wondered if they were brother and sister.

Terrance had to admit, when he had first stepped into the Rawsbrudge Theatre a matter of minutes earlier—still tasting a few uncomfortable grains of the coffee he'd downed too fast on his way back up from the Underground—he'd thought that the two figures standing up on the stage were naked beneath those trench coats. But, having caught a glance between the buttons of the female actor's coat, he could confirm that she—*at least*—wore *something* beneath.

Terrance made a point of *not* arriving late to these speculative shows at the theatre—the ones from which producers would choose to commission for anything from regional tours, to full-blown West End productions.

Needless to say *The Unlikely Bibles* was *unlikely* to find its place in the cultural milieu on the West End.

But there *was* something.

Certainly *something*.

Terrance tilted his head to the side. He looked over the leather seats, all of them scuffed up after year-upon-year of audiences taking in the spectacles here at the Rawsbrudge. As he looked along the row of seats, he caught Adam Knotworn's eye.

Adam, in response, gave Terrance the flicker of a smile.

A wink.

Yes, that was right.

How could Terrance have forgotten?

The *bet!*

As always happened following these morning speculative theatre sessions, a whole group of them—of the *producers*—would relocate to a delightful independent Italian restaurant located on the street corner.

What would follow—for most of the producers, though not for Terrance—was far too much wine. A week ago, on a Friday, Adam had managed what Terrance had thought to be the impossible. Despite *years* of refusal to touch so much as a drop of alcohol during the working week—let *alone* at lunchtime on a working day!—Adam had managed to get Terrance to have a glass of white wine with his pasta and green pesto.

What followed, at least to Terrance's remembering, was a warm sort of feeling descending over his brain. A sort of *unknotting* sensation. As if, after all this time—after all this 'living'—Terrance had finally found a way to 'let go'.

Following *that* lunchtime, Terrance could quite see how alcohol made mincemeat of alcoholics.

He hadn't drunk since that Friday.

Not even his regulation glass of red wine on Friday evenings.

Or the optional glass at lunch on Saturday or Sunday.

Although the overbearing reason that Terrance hadn't wanted to have another drink was because of the sheer sensation, another reason could be sourced from what had gone on *after* he had drunk said glass of wine.

They had got chatting—as they always did—about the acts they'd observed that morning. And, particularly, about the variety and *oddity* of them.

This sort of chatter, at least for Terrance, ranged from the downright playful, to the outright *obscene*—sometimes with a lot of 'sexual' innuendo . . . the producers' lunch was a mainly *male* affair, after all.

Terrance wasn't *totally* sure from where Adam had come up with a 'bet', but it had happened all the same.

With his hand outstretched across the table, Adam had challenged Terrance to find the *oddest* group of players he could and for him to take them on, as a kind of manager.

Adam would do the same.

And whoever made the most amount of money would be the winner.

It sounded simple enough to Terrance, and, in that moment, as he'd reached across to shake on the bet, he'd thought it the *easiest* thing in the world.

He had had no thought for the consequences.

For what was *at stake*.

Quite simply, Adam had stated that the loser would be forced to put on an hour-long, one-man show for the producers in the Rawsbrudge.

And, while Terrance had been flying high on that glass of white wine, he had only seen that as a minor detail.

An *amusing* moment for every producer involved as Adam took to the stage and turned on his one-man comedy routine.

That Adam, he really *was* built for the stage.

It was only afterwards, in the sobriety of the early evening, that Terrance had realised that what had gone on at lunch had been a ruse. That the other producers, having built Terrance up as a kind of 'square' had contrived a way, between themselves, of getting Terrance up on that stage so that they might laugh at him for an hour solid.

Terrance had *terrible* stage fright.

As he had found out when he'd attempted to be an actor in his younger years, before finding that the administration was much more his bag.

Still, a bet was a bet.

Nothing Terrance could do to change it now.

If he backed out he would look a fool.

Worse, he would lose his reputation of being an *honest* man.

And nothing mattered to him *more* than his reputation.

Terrance brought himself back to the present with several blinks of the eye. He broke off his stare with Adam, though he knew there would be no backing out now. Terrance had never had any sort of a poker face. Adam had seen, quite clearly, that Terrance thought this pair on stage right now—with their trench coats and wire-mesh cart filled with pamphlets—just about the oddest act he had ever come into contact with.

Terrance glanced along the seats to Adam, and then, sensing that *The Unlikely Bibles* were close to wrapping up, he got up and strode off to the backstage area.

2

A COUPLE OF UNSHADED BULBS illuminated the backstage area.

Kept it from *complete* darkness.

Like backstage areas always did, it stank of disinfectant and floor polish.

Terrance could taste a little of his peanut butter and toast breakfast rising back up his throat. It was funny. Even though he was a producer now—had been for several years—the *proximity* to the stage still got to him. It sent nervous wriggles through his muscles.

Right down to his toes.

Was that the feeling of failure?

Of knowing that he *couldn't*—no matter how hard he tried—do something that he loved so dearly?

One of the 'Unlikely Bibles' delivered a parting word of thanks to the audience.

There was a smattering of applause through the theatre.

It lasted no more than three seconds.

And then it was replaced by the sound of creaking floorboards as *The Unlikely Bibles* strode their way towards the side of the stage.

To where Terrance stood.

Terrance clasped his hands together. Felt the sweat act as an adhesive. He looked over the audience—his fellow producers—extremely briefly. Even the act of simply *looking out* at the audience got his head in a spin. It sent him back . . . back to That Evening on the stage . . . fully rehearsed . . . and yet . . . and yet . . . the words just wouldn't come.

So wrapped up was Terrance in his memories, that he almost

missed the *rustle* of the beige trench coats passing him by. He snapped himself out of his daze. "Uh, excuse me?"

The man and woman: the two-person act which consisted 'The Unlikely Bibles;' stared back at him. What struck Terrance the most were their dour expressions. How they remained entirely stone-faced as he told them of his intentions.

To take them to the stage.

Usually, one of Terrance's favourite parts of his job was getting to deliver the news to the aspiring theatre production, that he—*a producer*—was interested in bringing their dream to life. This time, though, it was only with a pair of nonchalant shrugs, a pair of dead-eyed pouts, that an act took him up on his offer.

Terrance made the arrangements to meet them later on that day.

To discuss *technicalities*.

On his way back out of the theatre, Terrance didn't feel any sense of joy. He felt nothing at all, really. Just empty inside. A vague sense of fear and foreboding waiting in the wings. That one-man spot yawning wide open in his mind like a bottomless abyss.

He didn't run into Adam until he had got out into the lobby and, in retrospect, if Terrance had been thinking straight, he would've maybe asked one of the stage hands to allow him out through one of the back doors.

But, then again, perhaps it was also a sense of dogged, male pride.

That he *wouldn't* back down in the face of a challenge.

Have his reputation brought into question.

The lobby floor was sticky, as was *always* the case in theatres, no matter what consistency of bleach—or whatever it was—the cleaners decided to use. As Terrance set one foot in front of the other, the sole of his shoe made a dry *thwacking* noise.

The air carried a waft of vomit and sawdust.

There were *always* those theatre audiences who simply *could not* contain themselves.

Quite literally.

When Terrance eyed the darkened—very much closed—refreshments counter, he caught himself eyeballing, for several moments, an advertisement for instant coffee.

That sent a bitter thrill through his mouth.

A slight *buzz* through his tongue.

Adam, as always, looked crisp and neat, his black hair slicked to the right-hand side with a healthy helping of gel, or wax, or whatever nastiness men used to keep their hair in the 'right' place . . . Terrance, quite frankly, had never quite been able to abide this intangible law, and he was actually quite proud of his bird's nest hair which grew wild and light-brown and *naturally*.

Today, Adam wore a crimson tie over the top of his crisp, clean white shirt. The trim of his suit, as always, was sharp: well-managed . . . just like his acts.

His cologne was *overpowering*.

He smirked at Terrance and held out his hand.

Immediately, Terrance's mind sketched back to that fateful handshake in the Italian restaurant. And, for a second, he had to remind himself that, in actual fact, this was only a greeting and that no strings were attached to this particular handshake.

And so he shook.

Adam flushed his eyebrows. "Interesting, interesting," he said, in a way which seemed almost like laughter to Terrance's ears. "You think that they'll win you the bet, then, I suppose?"

"I think so," Terrance replied.

"Good, good," Adam said, glancing around.

This habit wasn't one which Terrance had much trouble with.

In the circles he inhabited, people were *always* looking around, seeing who else might be on the scene. Even Terrance, though he liked to uphold himself as a model of manners, probably did it.

It was just business.

Thinking that he should put up a little more of a front—show Adam that he wasn't, *necessarily*, going to be a pushover—Terrance put in, "You haven't found an act for yourself just yet?"

Adam gave a shrug. "I'm giving it time."

And, just then, Adam's inside-jacket pocket buzzed.

He produced his mobile from within.

Gave Terrance an apologetic smile and answered.

3

THE CAFÉ where Terrance arranged to meet *The Unlikely Bibles* was named *Lemon Teas*. That was somewhat odd seeing as the café appeared to specialise in coffee rather than tea, though they *did* sell a special form of lemon tea . . .

Terrance ordered a black coffee and then took up his position at a no-nonsense, small, round table near to the door of the café. He did up the buttons of his suit jacket, as was his professional code; and then he clutched his hands on the surface of the —*surprisingly clean*—walnut table.

For a few moments, Terrance just absorbed the feel of the café. The warmth which resonated from behind the counter. He breathed in his coffee, those rich—*bitter*—notes and he realised, quite soon, that he was shaking.

Whether it was from a caffeine overdose, or memories of the bouts of stage fright in his youth, he really had no idea at all.

If it *was* caffeine overdose then he made sure of it by taking a few sips of his coffee.

'The Unlikely Bibles', still dressed in their stage garb—or what Terrance had *thought* to be their stage garb—wandered on in through the door to the café.

As Terrance considered the male member of 'The Unlikely Bibles', saw that he was trawling along the wire-mesh cart, with the pamphlets that they'd used on stage, he scolded himself for not having asked after their names.

That, really, was *Schmoozing 101*.

Still, there would be time for that now.

Neither member of *The Unlikely Bibles* ordered anything from the café counter. And Terrance didn't notice either one of them shoot him a glance—*even to check that he was there*—before they took up the pair of unoccupied seats at his table.

Terrance settled in his chair. He laid one of his elbows on the chair back in a carefree gesture he had learned would communicate *Ease* and *Comfort*, after so many years in and around the arts business world.

The gesture had no discernible effect on the male or female component of 'The Unlikely Bibles'.

Terrance removed his elbow from the chair back.

Instead he laid his hands, clutched tightly together, in his lap.

"Well," Terrance said, putting on a smile, "I can't get you anything to drink at all?" He paused for a moment, feeling both the woman and the man's eyes upon him. "I'm buying."

No response.

Terrance felt a numbness take hold of his buttocks. He shifted a little in his chair, hoping to get shot of it.

No dice.

"So," Terrance began again, "I enjoyed the show you put on for us." He broke out into—*even to him*—an uneasy smile. "Though I'm sure that much is apparent since I asked the two of you here."

Getting no response this time either, Terrance's attention shifted downwards, to the wire-mesh cart, partially concealed beneath the table. When Terrance tilted his head around, trying to get a better look at the pamphlets within, the male component of *The Unlikely Bibles* shifted the cart, protectively, closer to his leg. And concealed it completely beneath the table.

Terrance *did* have the chance to read the cover of one of the pamphlets, though, before the cart disappeared totally.

Like the name of the act, the pamphlet was titled:

The Unlikely Bibles.

Terrance glanced up at *The Unlikely Bibles* once more, as if they might've transformed, in the past few seconds, into more easily relatable human beings.

Nope.

That pair of blank, endless gazes still present.

Terrance wondered if these people had any sort of gauge of just how they were appearing to *him:* a producer. The very fact that they'd *got* a gig at all at the Rawsbrudge surely clued them in on that.

Then again, Terrance *had* met some extremely 'artistic' types in his time, which was to say those who didn't really seem to *exist* in the real world, or be constrained by the *rules* of the real world.

They were almost all, without exception, dead by the time they turned twenty-seven.

Was that what Terrance was looking at here?

A pair of *future* dead artists?

Well, if he wanted to get really down into the nitty-gritty of it all, then he had to acknowledge that *everybody* was going to be dead at some point.

Just that some would up clogs a little earlier than others.

He tried to turn his focus back to this—for want of a better word—meeting.

"The point is, see," Terrance went on, "I *wish* to take on management of your act, to push you into getting some venues, to finding you an audience." He looked between 'The Unlikely Bibles', trying to discern *some* emotion that wasn't overwhelming indifference. "How does that sound?" he said.

There was a long—*long*—silence, and, in the end—*miracle of all miracles*—the male component of *The Unlikely Bibles* responded.

"We want followers."

Pleased to have bled a word out of *either* of them, Terrance grinned back like an idiot—probably *nodded* like an idiot too—and then said, "Terrific—just *terrific!*"

4

I T WAS A WEEK LATER before Terrance thought it prescient to drop in on one of *The Unlikely Bibles'* rehearsals.

He had arranged for them to have an attic space, off a back road, just around the corner from the Rawsbrudge Theatre, on the pretence—or so he told himself—that the duo might feel more comfortable to be nearby where they had first caught his attention.

Perhaps, in any case, it might elicit *some* sort of emotion in them.

Even if it was just more indifference.

The most overwhelming feature of clambering up the creaking, old, splintered staircase and to the attic space, was the complete silence which dominated.

Now, having already seen a performance of *The Unlikely Bibles*, he had—by no means—been expecting a balls-out thesp-fest. But, at the same time, he hadn't bargained for there to be a complete absence of noise whatsoever.

When Terrance did reach the attic space, when he peeped in around the doorframe, he had convinced himself that—like so many of the entitled artists he'd run into over the course of the years—*The Unlikely Bibles* had flown off the proverbial handle; were lying in some back alley somewhere, in a heroin-induced coma.

Spittle drooling from their lips.

Perhaps they were naked . . .

Terrance caught his mind as it got wandering, and fixed his attention back on the spectacle before his eyes. They were here. Yes, that was well and good. He could see them *there*, both of them standing on the raised platform towards the back of the attic space, the golden sunlight gleaming through the large window which faced down into the street.

Terrance could see the dust particles floating about in the draught, in the ray of light. He could feel those same dust particles floating up his nostrils. Tickling his nostril hairs. It gave him a slightly bloody taste at the back of his mouth. He padded the pockets of his jacket, located his handkerchief and then bundled it in his fist, ready to administer as necessary.

But the sensation held off.

For now.

When Terrance had rounded the doorway, he'd been hoping that he wouldn't disturb *The Unlikely Bibles*. The very last thing he wanted to do was get in the way of some gushing creative flow. And, it seemed—at least to his eye—that he had succeeded in that ambition.

However, well, how should Terrance put it to himself . . . *The Unlikely Bibles*—both of them—were standing up on the elevated platform, the two of them, to Terrance's eye, just staring at one another.

Oh, they were wearing their beige trench coats.

And the cart carrying the endless *Unlikely Bibles* pamphlets was present.

In short, all appeared as it had done at the Rawsbrudge.

But there was, well, *no talking*.

No *action* either.

Whereas back down at the Rawsbrudge, the two members of *The Unlikely Bibles* had stood up on the stage, facing the audience almost—*but not quite*—glowering while the male component —*damn, how had he still not asked after his name?!*—read from one of the pamphlets.

Now, though, nothing.

Silently, Terrance wondered to himself just how long they'd been standing like that.

He thought about calling out to them.

Announcing his presence.

But the two of them were so . . . *focussed* . . . staring at one another.

Beige trench coats.

Cart between them.

The male component with one of the pamphlets dangling from his fingertips.

And Terrance caught the distinct impression that—really—it was probably better for him just to let himself out quietly.

There were some mysteries of the arts which he couldn't identify—*never mind* fathom—and he had no intention of imposing himself on whatever alchemy might be taking place here.

He returned to the, rather fetching, *Lemon Teas* café to ponder another of his acts.

5

OVER THE COURSE of the next week or so, Adam informed Terrance of the rules. He put them into a more fleshed-out form. He told Terrance that they would both be permitted ten performances: no-holds barred there; and that once the ten performances were over, the takings would be counted and the winner declared.

It all sounded so fair.

So *reasonable* to Terrance.

He had shaken on it.

And so, why was Terrance so riled by the whole ordeal?

Because, he reasoned with himself, he couldn't quite face the prospect of *losing*.

That one-man act.

That *performance* before the other producers.

That *utter* humiliation.

Terrance hadn't had the luck of being sat in the Rawsbrudge Theatre when *Adam* chose his act, so he made a point of going along to the first performance which Adam put on.

It was a chilly night—a chilly night for summer—and Terrance got out his thick, lambswool overcoat for the occasion. He even put on a pair of leather gloves.

The performance was taking place at The Dilge—a tight, but well-known venue—and Terrance got himself there about an hour before the raising of the curtain.

He read the posters, saw Adam's production company— *TWOTS & Co.*—logo splashed at the bottom of them all. He glanced over the name of the act:

Runny Seven

Well, not much Terrance could make of that.

He looked to the group of men and women on the poster.

All of them dressed in eighties-era running gear.

Short shorts.

White socks drawn well up shins.

Headbands aplenty.

All of the players wore those inane children's-television-presenter smiles.

In fact, Terrance was certain that he recognised a pair of them *as* children's television presenters. Once when he had been charged with babysitting his niece for a weekend—Good Lord, *never* again—he had ended up in the firing-line of *morning* television.

Children's morning television.

It had been some show about singing numbers.

Counting from one to twenty, and then all the tens up to a hundred.

And *that* song.

Why, it was *still* lodged in his brain.

Like a stray bullet from a long-ago fought war.

Terrance cleared his mind of such unpleasantness.

Turned his attention to the evening ahead.

To the *entertainment*.

Terrance found his seat on the front row.

Although he hadn't intended it, he had ended up there.

Right at the front.

Terrance supposed that—if Adam chose to interpret it so—it might be seen as a sign of aggression. And, if there was any image that Terrance wished to project of himself, it was *certainly not* as some kind of aggressor.

However, Terrance's manners, again, played into conflict with the Fates, because he couldn't quite bring himself to rise up out of his seat and go find another, further back in the theatre. He had his ticket for *this exact seat* and he saw no reason in, no doubt, bothering the usher—even the *players*, perhaps looking on from the side of the stage—by taking himself off to sit in a seat which hadn't been assigned him.

And so he sat tight.

In his front-row seat.

The theatre wasn't close to being full.

Getting in an inconspicuous look around the theatre, Terrance saw that it was only just over a quarter full—*if that*—and he couldn't help the smile from breaking out on his lips. Because —*just maybe*—he might have a chance of beating Adam.

Perhaps the popularity of *The Unlikely Bibles* was a wave, just waiting to rise, and . . .

But the performance was beginning.

Terrance gripped the arms of his chair tightly as he observed— one by one—the *Runny Seven* emerge onto the stage.

They were putting on a sort of farcical-hiding routine.

Each member of the *Runny Seven* would step out onto the stage, hiding their face with their hands; they'd then skulk about for a while, getting up to high-jinks, and whatnot—this consisted mostly of the flicking of ears, the tapping of shoulders, or, in one case, the pinching of bottoms.

There was no speaking.

It was an entirely *slapstick* performance.

And—*thank God!*—it was over in forty minutes flat.

A small applause followed, and Terrance got himself up from his seat. He wandered his way along the aisle, already thinking about the nightcap he was about to dose himself with from the theatre bar. He hadn't got even ten percent of the way to the bar when he heard—*loud and clear*—Adam's voice calling after him.

Terrance turned around to see Adam up in one of the boxes which hung at the side of the stage. At first, he did a mock royal wave to Terrance, and then he made a drinky-drinky gesticulation before pointing off in the direction of the bar.

It seemed like it wouldn't be a *peaceful* nightcap, after all . . .

Although the concept of a nightcap was somewhat alien to Terrance—for someone who kept his alcoholic cravings well in check—he found it quite refreshing to touch the cool rim of the glass to his lips.

And to breathe in the thick scent of lime and gin.

The tonic water seemed to settle his stomach somewhat.

He felt the bubbles all sorting things out *down there*.

It was a shame that the same couldn't be said for the company.

Adam blabbered on endlessly, flapping his arms about here and there, speaking about this and that. And Terrance wryly observed that, for Terrance's one gin and tonic, Adam ordered three Bloody Marys.

Considering the way that the gin was *already* sailing up to Terrance's head, he couldn't quite grasp how Adam seemed to take all that *vodka* within the Bloody Mary in such good spirits.

Without so much as a blush to his cheeks, or a slur to his speech.

These, Terrance supposed, were the hallmarks of the Drinker.

Thank *God* he had tapped all those habits on the head back when he'd been a fledgling actor. Just to *think* about where he might be today if he had given in as easily as Adam obviously had.

But, then again, Terrance *was* drinking on a weekday.

And he made a mental note to himself that 'it always started with one'.

Adam was in the process of ordering his fourth Bloody Mary when Terrance put it to him that he should really be getting going. That it was a little late now, and that Terrance had to put the finishing touches to *The Unlikely Bibles'* first performance.

There was an element of bending the truth present in that

particular statement, since Terrance hadn't yet nailed down the venue, and he hadn't returned to another rehearsal following the fateful first one he had attended.

But he was convinced that his intentions were good.

That he was getting out of the way of the steamroller of alcohol.

Adam just flapped him away with a wry smile, and settled in—apparently—to drink his fourth Bloody Mary alone.

6

TERRANCE GOT *The Unlikely Bibles* booked into a place a little way off Jourdicker Street.

Somewhere called the Tootinar Theatre.

Some place that Terrance had never heard of.

And it had been an uphill struggle to get them booked in there.

Despite Terrance's sharp suit—his *sharper* contacts about town —he had had trouble getting in touch with anybody who might give *The Unlikely Bibles* a chance.

It was almost as if Adam had been about town *poisoning* the water against them.

But Terrance knew that was only ridiculous.

This was just a little bet, whatever it was that Adam stood to gain from it.

Both he and Adam had their day jobs to attend to.

What Terrance thought he wanted to say was that he really had no time to dedicate to the sabotage of *Runny Seven*. So why should Adam have time to dedicate to the sabotage of *The Unlikely Bibles?*

Just didn't make sense.

The theatre was small, but they packed the place out.

In the end, it was hard to compare just how much they took that first night of *The Unlikely Bibles'* performance from simply looking about the seats. All the complicated promotional price tricks the venue was pulling only made the task harder.

What was harder still was the audience reaction.

It turned out that the Tootinar Theatre's main audience consisted of drunk students and the homeless. And, as Terrance stood on the doorstep of the place, a cup of coffee clasped in his hand, he watched several of the staff from the ticket office just *giving* seats away for the night's performance.

That had been the warning.

For what he was to expect.

Terrance sat in his seat, located discreetly towards the back of the theatre—he hadn't wanted to put off *The Unlikely Bibles* by staring them right in the face from the front row. As Terrance felt all the—*surely*—rusted-up springs within his chair all slinking about beneath his weight, he observed the nudging and giggling going on the audience.

That was among the students.

And it was to say nothing of the sleeping happening in and around the homeless.

Terrance turned his mind back to the stage.

And to *The Unlikely Bibles.*

7

B Y THE TIME *The Unlikely Bibles* got through, Terrance had
counted half a dozen cans of drink, four mashed-up wads of
paper from takeaway food, and a pair of underinflated condoms
that had been tossed—*unceremoniously*—at the night's entertainment.

Terrance was certain, each time he observed the silhouette of a
new projectile arcing for the stage, that the male and female
component of *The Unlikely Bibles* would merely shuffle off out of
the spotlight.

But they stayed put.

Centre stage.

Terrance watched on as each and every word tumbled on out
of the male component's mouth—as he jabbered his way through
the pamphlet which he held in his hand, and as the audience
—*apparently*—didn't hear a word.

Didn't even think to *listen* to so much as a word.

Terrance felt bad for *The Unlikely Bibles*, and what they'd had to
put up with here, tonight at the Tootinar . . . but, then again, he
couldn't quite observe any sort of a change in their exterior. They
didn't seem to feel strongly one way or the other about the reaction they had elicited from their audience.

Still, Terrance himself was *extremely glad* to watch the curtain
tumble down, without so much as a cue from *The Unlikely Bibles*,
once about an hour and a quarter had passed by.

Terrance supposed it was as much to spare the cleaners as to
spare the act itself.

As Terrance got up from his seat, he managed to avoid a bullet,
catching sight of Adam's figure rising up out of the audience. He
made a point of going in the opposite direction to him. He *really*

wasn't in the mood for a 'nightcap' this evening, which was to say nothing of having to endure a conversation with Adam.

Needless to say, Terrance did notice Adam shaking his head—and *laughing?*—as he shifted on out of the theatre, on the heels of the other audience members.

Terrance decided to head backstage to make sure everything was okay.

When he got back there, and he looked over the pair from *The Unlikely Bibles*, saw that their beige overcoats were now stained with a combination of beer, and food grease and that each of them had more than a couple of emergent bruises about their faces—where they'd each been caught by a headshot—Terrance couldn't help but feel a sharp twisting in his stomach. And he thought about calling the whole thing off.

He thought that was for the best.

And perhaps he *would've* if it hadn't been for one minor detail.

The Unlikely Bibles—both components—were smiling from ear to ear.

Equally unphased by what had just occurred.

About how their 'act' had gone down like the proverbial lead balloon.

Terrance really couldn't think what to make of it.

Other than to assume that the two of them were somewhat mad.

Then again, what had Terrance assumed from the start?

Thinking that he should at least see if this was some sort of a sturdy front for the emotional rot which'd set in underneath, Terrance looked to the male component—the *speaking* component of *The Unlikely Bibles*—and he said, "Are you quite all right?"

He struck a tone which, he ensured, wouldn't come across as overly concerned. That wouldn't make it sound like Terrance was putting any sort of a judgement on the night's performance.

Because it was almost impossible to square just what the act expected from the audience reception, and what Terrance might've observed.

He thought about how he'd dealt with—*did deal with*—acts which were ecstatic at having riled the audience up, at having made three quarters of them leave by the end of the show. And then there were the acts who would be despondent that they'd got three rounds of standing ovations. Left every man, woman and —*God forbid!*—child in tears by the time the curtain came furling downwards.

Terrance had never quite got either of those reactions.

And he didn't get *The Unlikely Bibles'* reaction now, though, he had to admit, he was somewhat *less* surprised than he would've been for a different act.

Seeing as there was certainly the *unconventional* slant to *The Unlikely Bibles.*

Realising that there was nothing more for him to say, Terrance left *The Unlikely Bibles* in peace.

He stomped on off into the night.

Back home.

8

THE NEXT NINE PERFORMANCES proceeded along a pretty similar track.

So similar, in fact, that Terrance *did* find himself considering that Adam really had put time and effort into sabotaging *The Unlikely Bibles*.

Had he gone about town telling them just what *The Unlikely Bibles* were all about?

Kept venues from booking them?

Terrance supposed not.

After all, *The Unlikely Bibles* were not at all what might be considered a *conventional* act, and, as such, they had no ready-made audience.

The same couldn't be said for *Runny Seven*, who, with their slapstick, could open their act for children. That allowed them those all-important Saturday morning slots. Those times where all the desperate mothers would show up, looking for *something* to free their hands of their children. And though Terrance didn't attend any more of their performances—to do so would've been, undoubtedly, *depressing*—he picked up bits and pieces of how they were getting on.

And they were getting on *Very Well Indeed*.

As for *The Unlikely Bibles?*

Well, they had, so far, lost a great deal of money.

Of Terrance's money.

But there was nothing to be done.

Terrance simply *had* to continue.

Before Terrance knew it, the tenth performance rolled around. One more time. And he was thankful, although the audience didn't realise it would be *The Unlikely Bibles'* final performance, that every man and woman watching on was patient. That during the hour and a half that the male component of *The Unlikely Bibles* blabbered on about the contents of his pamphlet, they all sat there, eyeballing the stage, *waiting* for some punchline, no doubt. And then, when the curtain came down, and they saw there wasn't one, there wasn't so much as a single voice of protest, just a shrug of the shoulders and a general shuffling for the exits.

Glad to be given permission to head for the theatre bar.

Terrance didn't go backstage that night.

Because he had preparatory work to get done.

He needed to plan for his one-man show.

9

ON THE MORNING of his one-man show, Terrance found himself facing off with the bathroom mirror. A bottle of brandy sat in the sink before him. Its cap screwed on tight from the last time he had poured it over a Christmas pudding.

He stared himself in his sad, pale-brown eyes.

Tried to see something beneath.

To see who it *was* staring back at him.

And he came up with no answers.

By the time Terrance had got himself dressed, he had dosed himself up with a good helping of the bottle. That, at least, seemed to take care of his shaking. He had been brushing up on his notes for such a long time the night before.

Trying to get all those *elusive* lines into his head.

He thought he'd finally managed it.

Hoped he'd finally managed it.

As Terrance tightened his tie about his neck, he fantasised—just for a couple of blissful moments—that it was a noose. And that he was about to tie the other end of it to one of the sturdy beams which hung down from the rafters of his historical town house.

But that would be shameful.

Too shameful for him to take.

A suicide in the family took *generations* to get over.

And he couldn't bear being selfish.

Not thinking how his death might affect his sister.

She would no longer have an inadequate babysitter to call upon, for one . . .

No, Terrance needed to go through with this performance.

Whatever it might mean to his physical health.

Once Terrance arrived at the Rawsbrudge Theatre, he knew

that there would be no turning back. Already, his fellow producers had spotted him. They knew that he had shown his face here.

Wasn't that *something?*

Couldn't he have *a little* respect?

Even though he had lost the bet?

Terrance didn't mingle with his fellow producers, but like the most serious of artists, he slipped off into the backstage area. Where he could wait in the wings.

His mind uncorrupted before his looming performance.

It was as Terrance waited there, trembling now as the brandy began to wear off, that he noticed the presence of a pair of figures. He frowned hard, screwed up his eyes against the dark, trying to make sense of the shapes there.

In the end, he did manage to work out who they were.

Saw the shapes of those beige overcoats.

And the cart looming between them.

Today, though, they had a new object.

One which the female component of *The Unlikely Bibles* held.

It took Terrance another blink of the eye to work out just what it was.

And then he had it.

Another beige overcoat.

Draped over her arm.

Terrance breathed in deeply, flexed his shoulders back, thought about the act he had prepared. All those *unfunny* jokes which stretched on for an entire hour. He thought about all those awkward stares from the audience.

From his *colleagues.*

They would never—*ever*—allow him to forget this.

To forget that he was *never*—and *never would be*—an actor.

Rather than discreetly stringing himself up from one of the

rafters in his home, this was far more like a *public* hanging. There for all to see.

And there was no way out now.

The female component held the beige overcoat out to Terrance, and Terrance only hesitated once. Just for a moment. And then he knew that there was nothing else for it.

He took the overcoat off her.

Swung it about his shoulders.

Did it up.

Then he looked to *The Unlikely Bibles*.

They looked back at him.

And they were one and the same.

SPORTS AGENT

NATHAN CLARKE pressed his thick head against the brick wall. "I'm not doing it."

"All right, all right." James Butler held out the palms of his hands and backed away.

James couldn't believe Nathan was turning down this opportunity. It was money: plain and simple. He decided on a different approach. "Why don't you want to do it?"

Nathan looked him in the eye and James saw the deep drive and determination staring back at him: 'Fighting spirit' or whatever you wanted to call it. Such a shame his body couldn't keep up with the ambition. All his clients reacted the same way, so predictable.

Nathan looked to the cameras on the race track. "It's humiliating."

"But, Nathan, think about your family."

"My wife left me," Nathan said. "I slept in the car last night."

James sucked his teeth, tapped his foot and hissed, "Jesus," under his breath.

The lives of these brutes fell apart at the end of their careers. That was where he came in. He had the job of milking their images as long as possible. The agency took twenty percent and, of that twenty percent, James took half. All those ten per cents had added up over the years. Those ten per cents bought his Japanese-style house, his Porsche, his kitchen. Hell, they probably bought his wife too.

He patted Nathan on the shoulder and thrust his £2,000 computer-designed smile in his direction. "Nathan, there comes a time in our lives when we have to say 'yes'."

Nathan looked away.

Was he crying? Jesus, he couldn't deal with that right now. The camera crew wanted to wrap up in the hour and they'd have to redo Nathan's make-up.

"You don't know what it's like." Nathan shook his head. "To compete and win . . . To win medals."

"I know." James maintained his smile, while taking a sneaky glance at the minute hand of his Rolex. "Wow, I forgot, I need to speak to the director."

"The director?"

"Yeah, yeah. The director." He winked. "Back in a sec."

James walked off to the crew. He had nothing to say to the director, of course. It was just one more step in this goddamn marathon of a process he'd concocted to deal with these washed up egos. He maintained a one-hundred-per-cent success rate using this method and saw no reason to think today would be any different.

With the same smile smeared across his face, he approached the director. He couldn't let the doubt show: professionalism, money. "Equipment ready to go?"

The director straightened up from inspecting the camera lens. "I think so, Nathan's ready?"

"Oh yeah, raring to go."

"Great, I'll call the rest of the team—they're round back."

James nodded. His smile hurt the corners of the mouth and he tried not to think about the lines ingraining themselves there permanently. They looked ghastly.

Last night he'd perused treatments. Elton, his boss, recommended Doctor Sparks, but James wanted to look around first. He thought of some possible jokes he could make with the surgeon before going into theatre. Perhaps, 'What do clowns and sports agents have in common?' He'd pause then hit him with the punch, 'They both have huge pockets!' He'd have to work on it, but they would laugh and he'd pay with his platinum credit card then they'd go their separate ways.

Capitalism was a beautiful thing.

James snapped out of his daze and noticed he was grinding his teeth again. That little habit worried him. He didn't want to add a psychiatrist to his list of monthly outgoings.

He looked over to the Portakabin where Nathan stood.

Perhaps it had been a mistake to come to a school field, far below the stature of a sportsman like Nathan Clarke. Sure, Nathan was stupid, but he was arrogant too. James respected that in a way.

Across the field, he glimpsed Nathan's muscular frame slide between the buildings. He was heading for the car park.

"Jesus!" James broke into a run. His shoes, designed for sleek offices and boardrooms, slipped a few times on the grass still covered in the late-September morning dew.

Skidding along loose gravel, he arrived at the car park to see Nathan sat in his TVR. He hadn't turned the ignition, but sat with both hands firm on the steering wheel.

James knocked on the passenger window. 'Communicate confidence', he thought. 'Confidence and assurance'.

Nathan wound down the window, but remained facing forward.

"Nathan, come on! We're filming soon."

"I can't do it. I've decided."

"But we've signed the contract."

Nathan turned to face him and James saw the fear in his eyes.

For a fleeting moment he felt sympathy for the big man. "Come on, let me in and we'll talk about it."

Nathan shook his head. "No, my mind's made up."

The engine roared into life and James felt a jolt of fear pass through his veins. "Nathan!" James's voice rose with tension. "Let me in!"

He watched in horror as Nathan released the handbrake and inched the car forward.

James ran round the car and stood in its path so there was nowhere for Nathan to go. The only other route out, behind him, was blocked by a fence then dense forest.

Nathan would have to run him over to get away.

Even as they stared each other out, James knew he would win in the end. He was a professional.

Sure enough, the engine rattled out of motion and the handbrake crunched back into place. James kept his hands placed on the car's bonnet.

They had bought the car together. He remembered the day in the showroom, seeing it there in the clean white space almost made him breakdown and buy it himself. When the salesman recognised Nathan, James stepped in to stop the man charging twice the list price. Good thing he was there. Sometimes he wished he had someone to look out for him, the way he looked out for others.

James smiled and made his way round to the driver's door. "We'll do something nice after. I promise."

Nathan sat still. Who knew what he was thinking?

James tugged at the door handle then tapped on the glass. "It's locked."

No response.

He tapped louder until it hurt his knuckles. "Nathan! Open up!"

The ignition burst into life once more, and with a single, swift motion the car pulled forward out of its space and swung out across the tarmac.

"Jesus!" James chased the car in vain then watched it drive off down the long road towards the gate.

Sweat moistened the back of his suit. What was he going to do? He bent over double, his hands on his knees, and tried to catch his breath.

After he'd removed the crease in his lapel, he walked back to the field. When he turned the corner, he saw the filming team—all set up and ready to go. He tried to turn back to the car park, half-thinking about chasing Nathan down the motorway in his Subaru. However, the director saw him and waved him over. There was nothing he could do now.

James pressed on his trademark smile and ventured over to the team.

As James got closer, the director's expression turned to one of concern. "Where's Nathan?"

James considered his answer. He didn't want to say Nathan was coming then not have him come back. *He'd* look the idiot then. But neither did he want to come across as the blundering agent, the one who'd lost his client. Those sorts of stories spread like wildfire through media circles. It was no joke. It could ruin his career. "He's getting a quick snack," James settled on.

The director frowned. "I thought he was ready to shoot."

"He will be, he will be." James felt like the nodding dog sat on his car dashboard—one of his wife's innovations.

The director didn't comment. He went back to his team and talked in their secret language. If they thought they made him feel excluded with their jargon they were wrong. Let them take a look at his bottom line for last month.

That would wipe the smiles from their faces.

His phone vibrated in his jacket pocket. He removed it and checked the display: 'Nathan C.'

He smiled. Hardly twenty minutes. He pressed the green button to accept the call and heard heavy breathing coming from the other end. "Nathan?"

There was a long pause. "Can you come get me?"

"Where are you?" James rubbed his temples with his other hand, looking forward to his massage tonight.

"Services at Knobworth Junction."

"Okay." James walked back towards the car park, secretly cursing the Subaru which was no match for a high-speed chase with Nathan's sports car.

James picked out Nathan's car immediately. The TVR was hardly inconspicuous parked across two disabled bays outside McDonald's. He glanced round, checking for any lurking journalists.

This was potential dynamite.

James opened up the passenger door of Nathan's car, and swept the half dozen burger boxes from the passenger seat onto the floor. He put on his *understanding* face—the one he used when he informed clients they wouldn't be offered a new contract by the agency (or any other agency for that matter). The 'You're Finished' face. He pointed to the burger boxes then said, "These won't help you win."

Nathan let out a long sigh and his stomach rumbled. All those hamburgers swimming around worked to destroy his physical perfection. "What's the point?"

"Of what?"

"Everything." Nathan looked at James with the same sad and distant look, as if this had never happened to anyone else on Earth.

James dreaded this stage of the conversation. He was an agent, not a psychiatrist, after all. "What about?" He searched for the words. "Family?" James bit his tongue, remembering Nathan had spent last night in the car.

However, Nathan remained calm and let the faux pas slide. "Yeah, but I let them down."

"How?"

"All I ever wanted was to be a hero. I wanted my kids to tell all their friends at school, 'Look! There's my dad, the great Olympic champion.'"

"They'll still say that."

Nathan snorted. "No they won't, they're too young. No one will remember in a couple of years' time."

"Make them remember," James said, improvising now. His phone was vibrating again, probably the director asking where they'd got to. "Show them pictures, videos, your medals."

"But it's not the same, from now on I'll always be a has-been." Nathan gave him a hangdog look. "Starting from today."

James thought about what the people passing by would be thinking: a huge, athletic guy dressed for track alongside a smartly dressed guy, inside a factory-fresh TVR—just your average upscale, gay breakup outside McDonald's. He thought again about his bank balance next month and felt much better. He laid a calming hand on Nathan's hulking shoulder, then said, "Come on big guy. Let's get you back to school."

Nathan wiped a tear from his face then turned to James and smiled. "Did you know you're my best friend?"

Although James was used to these declarations, part of the process, they always seemed to catch him off-guard, as if pulling at his inner-child's heartstrings—merging the ideas of 'friend' and 'client' into one impossible conglomeration. He put his hand on Nathan's knee and looked him in the eye. "Nathan, let's get you out there."

"Okay, but one thing."

"Anything," James said, his phone almost bursting out of his shallow pocket in its vibrating frenzy.

"Can you drive?"

"Of course, come on." James opened the door and made to get out.

"No, can you drive *my* car?"

For the first time that day James felt glad he'd brought the Subaru—not as likely to get nicked out here. In any case, he had first-party, second-party, third . . . well, his policy probably stretched to first boot in on the bugger who stole the damn thing.

He rested his arms on the top of the passenger door and looked in at the sad scene.

Nathan had the look of that same trapped young boy—all these guys had it—looking back with mournful eyes, wanting Daddy to tell them what to do next. "Anything for you, Nathan."

The camera sat upright in its static position and the crew gathered round for the introductory shots. James stood next to the director as they discussed the lighting, framing, and other such technical bullshit. Nathan's moping face caught his eye and James hoped he wouldn't break into another tantrum.

The problem had started when the director introduced the man in the dinosaur suit.

Things got more complicated when the director explained to Nathan it would be funnier for the show if he lost the race—comically tripped and lost his shorts, something along those lines.

James had watched Nathan's sharp smile disintegrate into a flabby frown, reminding him of a mongrel he'd had in his youth. His father had the animal put down in the end. It just hung around looking depressed, bringing everyone else down with it.

Dogs were meant to make you happy.

The director stood alongside Nathan, and the man in the dinosaur suit, giving out the final instructions. James had never seen the show before and thought the dinosaur resembled a knock-off Barney—purple and green. But, instead of the familiar toothy grin Barney sported, this dinosaur's expression was stuck in a grimace, as if it'd caught its foot in a bear trap.

It unsettled James to look at it.

Nathan caught James's eye and shook his head—time for him to step in.

"Five minutes and we can all go home," James said, reaching his arm round Nathan's giant shoulders, not quite able to touch his other arm.

They stood to one side with dinosaur and director out of earshot.

"My kids watch this show," Nathan said. "It'll be impossible to explain to them."

"Don't worry about it. Don't let them watch it."

This suggestion seemed to get through to Nathan. However, the brief enlightened look passed. "Why do I need to lose?"

"Because," James said with a reassuring grin, "it's funny."

"I don't get it."

James looked up to the sky for divine inspiration. No other

option, he wanted to get onto the golf course by four, before the corporate rats streamed on.

They ruined everything with their hipflasks and young-secretary caddies. He needed to take the hard line. "Listen, Nathan," he said with a raised voice. "You've signed the contract. You belong to us—so you're going to do whatever these nice men say."

Nathan nodded.

"We'll be done soon,." He patted Nathan on the bottom and strolled away, behind the camera.

He tapped his jacket pocket to hear the reassuring jingle of Nathan's car keys, safely tucked away next to his mobile phone.

No running away now.

"Cut!" the director called out. "That's a wrap."

James shook the director's hand and headed over to Nathan, his head bent down staring at the laces of his trainers.

The results were in.

The dinosaur had won.

As instructed, Nathan had tripped, inches from the finish line. It had looked quite convincing. If Nathan had been a bit more crooked (or perhaps a little brighter) he could've made an absolute bomb throwing races—if people bet on those types of races.

They'd rubbed it in, though, with the podium.

The director placed Nathan on the number two spot and filmed the dinosaur jumping up and down on the place above him with the gold medal strung around his neck.

Nathan didn't hide his emotion.

For Nathan's sake, James hoped it would come across better on television than live. He didn't want Nathan to come across as reluctant. It could kill Nathan's image and, more importantly, his *payday* if the production company couldn't use it.

Nathan signed autographs for some of the crew.

James sighed. Nathan was finished, done, out-to-stud; although James didn't quite have the heart to tell him. The wake, as they called it in the business, was scheduled for next week at four o'clock, Wednesday afternoon. The head of the agency, a lawyer and the personal agent, James, would sit down with Nathan and discuss ways to break up the contract. The timing of the meeting was strategic, designed so the agent went out with the client and painted the town all sorts of colours that night. Then, hopefully, the client would wake up the next day and forget what had happened in the meeting the day before.

But what about James Butler?

He would keep going, without expiration date. The only limitations on his career were heart attacks, car accidents or messy divorces—and all those were temporary setbacks.

Problems money could fix.

Death was the only real obstacle, but not much to do about that . . . not for now anyway.

Half an hour later, James sat in the car park watching Nathan's sports car drive down the slipway, away from the service station, and onto the motorway. He exhaled and smiled to himself as he turned the ignition.

Off to the golf course with an afternoon to kill.

ST CLERK'S

F ELICITY NADDLEWICK marched up the path to St Clerk's Progressive Education Centre for Girls. She wore a navy blue jacket over a long skirt of the same colour, which brushed her ankles. A pillbox hat rested on her tightly coiled hair. Her features appeared carved out of porcelain, only the light daubs of rouge giving the appearance of life. She rapped smartly on the door to the reception area, folded her hands over her waist and waited with her head tilted back slightly.

A blonde woman appeared at the door. She was dressed in a frumpy woollen pullover and had no make-up on. Her cheeks were flushed, as if she had been running, and her hair was bushy. She grinned in a slightly exasperated way. "You must be Felicity."

"Ms Naddlewick," Felicity said.

"Ah, well I'm Helen."

Felicity held out her hand to shake.

Helen stared at it a couple of moments, grinned again, then accepted it. She ushered Felicity inside and closed the door behind her.

Felicity ran her eyes over the reception. The whole place was an absolute mess. Papers piled up on a desk, shoes were scattered on the floor—as if their owners had just kicked them off and proceeded in socks—childish paintings and scrawlings plastered the walls.

Helen said, "Did the agency brief you on us?"

Felicity cleared her throat and turned her attention back onto Helen. She pursed her lips. "No."

Helen rolled up the sleeves of her pullover. The sleeves themselves rolled backed down almost as soon as she had rolled them up. No elastic. "Well, I'm sure you saw the sign outside."

"Yes."

"Right," Helen said, her fixed smile faltering a touch. "We're a progressive school. Parents send their children here to get a non-standard education so that they have the ability to express themselves in creative and unusual ways."

Felicity gave a silent groan.

Helen continued, "By 'non-standard' I mean that instead of learning maths from textbooks, they learn from real life situations. We take them out and put them through roleplaying so they can see what exactly it is they need. We don't have traditional English classes, but we encourage the children to find books which interest them and the role of the teacher—or educational facilitator, as we term it here—is simply to support and inspire." Helen cupped her chin in her hand. "We place a strong emphasis on individuality and the whole school is built around this model."

"And is it successful?"

Helen frowned. "I'm sorry?"

"The methodology. Do the girls go on to be successful members of society?"

Helen's familiar carefree glance returned, as if she had answered the same question a million times and had an all-powerful answer. "We're a new programme, you see, there's not really been enough time to look at the data."

"Right," Felicity said. "Where do you need me?"

Helen dug through a bunch of non-alphabetised folders before finally turning up one which she handed over to Felicity. "Here's the record of what they've been working on, along with the lesson plans."

Felicity flipped through the folder, pausing several times to scrutinise particularly ridiculous parts of the documentation. One sheet of paper was titled with a stick-on smiley face with a graph, presumably, indicating the various levels of happiness for each of the girls. They were all beyond the seventy-per-cent mark.

Helen said, "I'll show you to the room, shall I?"

Felicity remained silent as she followed Helen's lead, already dreading what might be in store for her today.

Yesterday she had been teaching at an inner city school, covering for a teacher who was in hospital after having been punched by one of the student's parents. While she, herself, had had no trouble at all with the class, bringing them into line with her usual rigid discipline, she had wished for a somewhat more relaxed assignment today.

But this would be a real challenge, after all what did children crave if it wasn't boundaries?

As they headed along the corridor several girls skipped by, cradling pots of paint or sketch pads to their chests. Some hummed tunes to themselves while another let out a shrill, piercing scream.

Felicity looked to Helen for any sign of a reaction, but she remained neutral walking onward, her arms swinging lightly at her side. Seeing that nothing would be done, Felicity called out to the girl in her short and snappy voice.

The girl stopped instantly. She spun on her heel, her sketchpad dangling down at her side and her mouth parted wide. She wore her hair in pigtails with little blue ribbons.

Felicity said, "Just what on *Earth* do you think you are doing?"

The girl looked to Helen, then back to Felicity. "I . . . I . . ."

Helen laid her hand on Felicity's upper arm. She was still grinning. "Please, Ms Naddlewick, we don't discipline the girls here. We must give them space to let out their emotions, to show us how they're feeling. It's damaging to reprimand them." She turned her attention on the girl. "Now, Cecilia, don't worry. You keep on doing what you feel you must."

Wary, the girl scanned Felicity and then took on her easy manner once again. She slipped out through the door, to the outside, without screaming, though.

Helen's smile faltered. "You'll get the hang of it before too long, don't you worry. Before I came here I spent ten years working in state schools. I know how all the traditional methods might well frown upon what we're doing here."

Felicity pressed her bloodless lips together and trotted on at Helen's side.

They arrived outside the classroom. Helen held the door open for Felicity, who passed through, keeping her head held high and her posture straight. If there was one thing that was all-important with children it was setting an example.

The girls, however, dashed from side to side of the classroom, playing some version of British Bulldog. As they went, they trampled school bags, coats and sketch pads. Their screeching laughter and pattering feet were almost deafening to Felicity.

Helen leant into Felicity, so that her mouth brushed her ear. Despite her proximity, she still needed to shout. "I'll leave you alone with them, okay?"

Before Felicity could make a return comment, Helen had backed away from her and was heading out of the door.

The girls continued their game, paying absolutely no attention to their newly arrived supply teacher. They bounded on their way, swept up in their own little worlds. One of the girls tripped over a bag and crashed in a heap. The other girls kept up their game, not bothering to stop for their fallen companion. The fallen girl curled up into a ball and sobbed to herself.

Felicity had seen more than enough. She clapped her hands together and let loose an enormous roar. "I think that's *quite* enough!"

A few of the girls stopped and examined her, but most of them continued on their way, giggling and sprinting. The fallen girl continued to cry from her place on the floor.

Felicity erupted a second time and she got the attention of the whole room. The few stragglers in the group, running back and forth also fell into line so that all the girls stood in their places, mouths slightly agape—just like the girl Felicity had told off in the corridor—as if something utterly shocking and out of place had just occurred.

"That's better," Felicity said, strutting up to the teacher's desk and laying her bag down upon it.

Chairs and desks were turned upside down, paper was scattered all over the place. The paintings which had been attached to the walls were dangling down or ripped. The girl who had been crying looked around and, seeing no one was going to help her to her feet, she got up herself, transfixed by Felicity just like all the others.

Felicity brushed herself down and eyed the girls. "Just what do you think you were doing?"

A girl sniffed. She was a couple of centimetres shorter than the others around her and she wore her hair cropped. She reminded Felicity of an oversized doll. "We were playing."

"We were playing, *miss*," Felicity said, correcting her.

The girl gawped.

"Who told you that that kind of behaviour is acceptable in school?"

The girl froze a few moments and then broke out of it. "Well everyone, miss."

"Every *who*?"

"Our teachers, miss."

Felicity nodded to herself and then waved her arm across the room, as if she were bearing a magic wand. "Clean this all up, then."

" 'Clean up', miss?" the same girl said.

"What's your name?" Felicity said.

"Jeanie."

"Right, Jeanie, if this room isn't spotless within five minutes then you'll all be in detention this evening."

There was a sustained gasp, and Jeanie spoke again. "But, miss, we don't have detention here. We can't have detention."

"We do while I'm here."

The girls muttered among themselves, and for a second Felicity was worried that they might call her bluff, decide that she really wasn't their teacher and that she would be overridden by whoever her superior was supposed to be, but then the girls rushed into action, buzzing around the room, setting tables and chairs right, scooping up litter.

In the meantime, Felicity tidied up her teacher's desk, which was just as bad as the rest of the room. When she attempted to prise open one of the drawers she was met with wads of paper keeping it blocked.

Five minutes later the classroom resembled some kind of an order. Felicity stood over them all, monitoring the finishing touches the girls put to the room, as they realigned their desks. As they took up their seats, Felicity could swear that behind their fearful expressions they were contented—glad some adult had decided to put them in their place, told them that what they were doing was wrong.

Minutes afterward they all sat at their desks, sheepishly staring at her with their glassy, glazed over eyes, completely lost and abandoned, no idea what they were supposed to do next—unsure over their role as school children.

This was where she came in.

Felicity ducked down and snapped open her bag. From it she withdrew a thick pile of worksheets and dished them out to the girls. Jeanie received hers and then raised her hand. "Miss? Miss?"

"What is it?" Felicity said, trying to inject kindness into her voice.

"What're we suppose to write with?"

"A pen or pencil will suffice."

"But, miss, I don't have a pen or pencil."

Felicity arched an eyebrow. "Are you joking?"

"No, miss, today I don't have any drawing. Just drama and painting. I didn't bring one."

Felicity suppressed a sigh and then looked over the rest of the room. "Anyone else not bring a pencil?"

Half a dozen hands shot into the air.

Felicity returned to her bag and dug out some more pencils, luckily she kept a pack of twenty stuffed inside for such occasions. Children were nothing if not predictable. There was always one who forgot his book, pencil or other basic piece of classroom anatomy.

Once all the pencils were dished out the girls worked away in silence, as if they remained in a state of shock over what had just happened to them, that they really were living out this strange situation with the teacher.

About half an hour later, there was a knock at the door and a parrot-like lady stuck her head in around the doorframe. "May I have a word, Felicity?"

"Ms Naddlewick," Felicity said, getting up from her seat, giving the girls a lingering glare so that they wouldn't break out into old habits the moment she turned her back.

They stood alone in the corridor. The lady wore a turquoise cardigan draped around her shoulders and a white blouse underneath. She wore her trousers tucked up tight to her waist. "I'm the head teacher here. Alexis."

"I see."

Alexis craned her neck and looked in through the window, into the classroom, where the girls continued to work hard on their assigned tasks. She turned her attention back to Felicity. "I understand that you're only temporary, and that you might well have been exposed to varying teaching styles in other places you have worked, but you must fall in line with our school principles. Do you have your lesson plans?"

"Yes."

"Then you know what is required of you."

Felicity remained silent, knowing that battles in school were never won amongst the staff—the children would make the difference.

Alexis continued, "The parents of these girls pay good money and they expect their children to receive exactly what they pay for."

"And what about when they grow up?"

"Sorry?"

"When they grow up, go out into the adult world."

Alexis unbuttoned then rebuttoned one of the cuffs on her cardigan. "Well, that's really none of our business, is it?"

"Oh, I beg to differ."

"Yes?"

"It will affect all of us. When we're in our nursing homes, these kids will be looking after us. Doesn't that frighten you at all?"

Alexis flinched, as if the mere word 'kid' were her trigger.

Felicity continued, "They'll be driving the buses, running our economy, staffing our hospitals. And this"—she threw up her hand to indicate the school—"is this really the way to help them adapt to those all-important roles?"

Alexis squinted and then rubbed her temple with her fingers. "We do things a little differently, here, Felicity."

"Ms Naddlewick."

"Yes, Ms Naddlewick. And while you're within these walls you shall abide by our rules, work alongside us to complete the school's mission. We have no need of social lectures or righteous speeches. Now, if you wouldn't mind returning to your post, and I shall return to mine."

Felicity gazed deep into Alexis's eyes, trying to get a handle on what she was attempting to achieve here, whether there was anything to salvage from her. She never gave up on an educator—they often surprised her, had a much better moral compass than might have been previously suggested.

Without another word, Alexis stalked her way up the corridor, back toward the head teacher's office.

Felicity took a deep, cleansing breath and then re-entered the classroom where, once more, chaos reigned.

A bell rang for break time around eleven o'clock in the morning. When the girls attempted to leap up from their desks, to bustle their way outside into the playground, Felicity stopped them in their tracks—informed them that due to their behaviour earlier they would sit in silence for five minutes.

There was a groan of protest but not one of them challenged her authority. And after the time had elapsed she sorted them into military lines and marched them out through the corridors, out into the playground. Once she had released them from her side, the girls launched off in various directions like heated-up atoms.

Felicity lined up beside the other teachers, all standing in a row. She was surprised to look over their faces, their expressions. Most of them had several wrinkles in their forehead and thinning hair.

They stooped backward, leaning against the wall. One of them had a cigarette dangling from her trembling fingers.

One of the teachers, a youngish woman with blond hair and a skinny face, eyeballed Felicity. A register dangling from her fingers revealed her name was, Yvonne. When she spoke there was a tenseness to her voice, like someone had wrapped a string around her vocal chords and drawn it tight. "How . . . how did you get them to behave . . . like that?"

In fact this woman reminded Felicity of a dog she had had in her childhood, where she had grown up on a farm. She recalled that one day it had got itself caught beneath a horse's hooves, and forever after it had treated everyone and everything with wariness.

Felicity snapped open her handbag and withdrew a box of mints. She offered them round the other teachers, and a few took advantage. With her own mint resting on her tongue, Felicity said, "The thing with children is that they require discipline and well-defined rules."

Yvonne shook her head with vigour. "No, no, that's completely against what we're about here. That doesn't work."

Felicity inspected her watch, seeing that it was getting toward the end of break time. She supposed they kept the break times short because the rest of the school day was nothing but relaxation anyway. Everyone knew the truth about what was going on but no one dared put it into so many words. "A school such as this cannot function. It will consistently turn out poorly-educated, ill-disciplined, emotionally-retarded girls."

"But . . . but," Yvonne said, "not emotionally-retarded. That's absolutely not what this school is about."

The other teachers' eyes almost rolled from their sockets.

Felicity said, "That's exactly what you're lining yourselves up to produce. Mark my words."

Yvonne shook her head another dozen times, as if denying it

over and over again might iron out the wrinkles on her face or grow her hair back thick and lush.

Felicity withdrew a nail file and spent the rest of break time, getting everything neat and tidy once again.

When the bell rang, Yvonne latched herself onto Felicity's arm and pulled herself close. "Please," Yvonne said, "you've got to tell me your secret. I'm afraid that I can't go another day with this, it's killing me."

Felicity smiled lightly and patted Yvonne on the hand. "Meet me for lunch and we'll talk."

As Felicity approached her classroom she had another run in with Alexis, who was lurking in the corridor, watching the girls file into the classroom tidily—like ducklings shuffling into the water under the mother duck's watchful gaze.

Alexis cocked her head to one side, waited for the last of the girls to get inside the classroom. "I can't help but notice the girls are not adhering to their structured plan."

Felicity shrugged. "They're adhering to my *structured* plan."

"Still, it's not quite in keeping with what we discussed, is it?"

"If you don't like my methods then you're quite free to complain to the agency. If you like, I can leave right now—"

"No," Alexis said, eyes bulging. "No, please don't go."

Felicity took in Alexis's suddenly changed aspect and considered the reasons for her quick change of heart. It struck Felicity that this school was just one step away from all-out rebellion—that just one unsupervised class might be all it would take to push the whole place over into revolution. And there was no telling what damage hundreds of rampant little girls might entail.

Felicity waited for Alexis to put so much into her own words, but she only kept up her frightened demeanour. After a few moments, when it became clear that Alexis had nothing to add,

Felicity slipped back into the classroom and resumed her day, just as she had planned it.

~

Lunchtime rolled around without much more drama. Felicity basked in the sound of other classrooms' girls, chattering away, running down the halls and screaming, while her own remained steeped in studious silence—only broken whenever a girl raised her hand and politely asked for help with a particular problem.

She led her class along the corridors, again in marching file, and she dismissed them when they got to the lunchroom. When she glanced around the room for somewhere to sit with her lunch, she noticed Yvonne waving at her frantically. She suppressed a groan and then fixed a smile on her face as she went over to go and join her.

Yvonne's expression was a mixture of panic and elation, like she had just been told great news but that it would mean her taking on a great amount of responsibility—and it frightened her. She almost jumped up from her seat when Felicity drew close. "Hello, hello! How are you?"

"Fine," Felicity said, taking her position on the table beside her.

"I . . . I told some of the other teachers."

"What?"

"About you giving me some tips, like what we talked about at break time. Is that okay?"

Felicity hardly had time to absorb the statements as Yvonne rattled them off, but she merely nodded and got on with eating her lunch.

As the other teachers slowly formed around her, Felicity got on with speaking, telling them all which she had observed at the school and how it needed to change—giving them the benefit of her supply teacher's experience. They listened attentively, with their heads bowed in toward her.

Once, as she held forth, she spotted Alexis at the other side of the hall. Alexis stared over before taking up her place at the end of one of the tables of girls, near to the door.

The lunch bell rang to signal the start of afternoon classes and Felicity collected up her girls and headed back to her own classroom.

Throughout the afternoon, the girls got on with their work and Felicity basked in the glow of a well-behaved class. She thought over the school, how it had been when she'd arrived that morning, and how it was now.

Things had certainly changed for the better.

At least in her classroom.

Halfway through the last lesson of the day, Felicity stopped writing on the whiteboard, realising a great change in the school atmosphere. No she wasn't dreaming. The entire place was silent. There wasn't a sound to be heard.

She finished up her explanation and then set her girls some problems to do, before venturing out into the hall and checking out the other classrooms.

All the way along, without exception, girls sat in their chairs, looking up at the board as the teacher explained. Just as Felicity had imagined, the girls here were absolutely desperate for some form of structure to their day, and now they had it.

Felicity returned to her classroom with a smile on her lips and she finished up the day giving the girls double rations of homework to only a small amount of sighing and headshaking.

As Felicity collected up her belongings, she spotted Alexis at the door, peering in at her like a woman possessed. Felicity draped her overcoat over her arm and then strode toward the door.

"That was quite something," Alexis said. "Nobody has made such an impact on this school, and so quickly."

Felicity gave her a slight smile and then slid past her, into the corridor.

"Ms Naddlewick?"

"Yes?" Felicity said, meeting Alexis's eye.

"Would you consider taking on a permanent position at St Clerk's?"

Felicity pursed her lips.

Alexis clenched her hands in front of her chest, as if in prayer. "Please. It would mean so much to us. I thought . . . I thought about what you said and it makes sense."

"What about the parents?"

Alexis chewed on her lower lip. "I'll have to make them understand." She brightened. "Maybe you can help me to tell them where we're going wrong."

Felicity shook her head. "No, thank you for the offer, Alexis, but I really don't think it's for me."

"But . . . but you can't think it's too difficult. You acted wonderfully today, whipped everything into shape."

"No, it's not the school, or anything to do with the children, it's just that I don't see myself in any one place. I'm a problem solver, and I like to take it one school at a time."

"Can't I say anything to have you reconsider?"

"No, I'm afraid not. There are plenty of failing schools out there and I have to be among them."

Alexis didn't respond, staring at the corridor floor as Felicity walked out of the school and their lives forever—onto the next challenge, leaving this one behind for others to pick and prune at until they got it more or less right.

WRECKING BALL

SAM GAX slammed down the phone. "Fuck!"

From his beach front mansion, he scanned the Welsh coastline spread out before him.

His eyes dropped to the back shore where his beach hut stood. The hut he and Chanel, his eighteen-year-old French girlfriend, had erected.

On rollerblades, Chanel skated over the mahogany floor to him. "What is the matter, beb-by?"

"Bloody wife!"

Chanel placed a hand on her hip and frowned. "Are you talking with 'er?"

"No." Sam threw up his hands. "Council just phoned. They're on their way to rip down the beach hut. Be here in half-an-hour." He paused. "I know she's behind it."

"That *beech*. When?"

"In about an hour." Sam shook his head. "Nothing for it now."

"You must do some'sing, Sam, you can't allow her to control your life."

"I know, I know." Sam's brain throbbed. Hadn't these kinds of stresses been the point of breaking up the band—to put an end to the incessant touring and craziness around him: the drink, the drugs, the sex . . . his wife?

Sam squeezed Chanel's bottom, peeping out from her silver hot pants and strolled off to consult his resident witch doctor, Eikia Wa.

The walls burst with framed Iron Frazzle records—gold and silver vinyl.

All those sales.

So many years. Sam couldn't tear his eyes away as he careened down the corridor.

Chanel had insisted he take down some of the photographs. The back-to-back soloing with his wife, the one of her whispering lyrics into the microphone under the glare of the spotlight, and the most famous one—the one they'd put on the third record cover—him and his wife kissing passionately under bright houselights after a storming set in Berlin.

Sam knocked on Eikia's door.

"Come in," Eikia said in his creaky, old-man voice.

Inside, an ultraviolet light illuminated scrawled walls. Sam thought it looked like someone had tried to use their semen to write graffiti—the words impossible to make out. Eikia had told him it was a London thing—strict, street symmetry, they called it, all the celebrities had it.

Sitting on a sequined cushion—a slight smile stitched onto his ebony face—Eikia said, "Erak Vomak."

Sam bowed his head and took up a cushion. "Erak Vomak. Mert Derdiger."

For about ten minutes, they sat—trying to ignore the intermittent roar of Chanel's roller skates as they meditated.

Sam concentrated hard on his problem. The beach hut, the love nest they'd installed last week. He needed options and needed them fast. But there was no rushing Eikia.

Spirituality didn't work that way.

Several minutes later, Eikia sat up and opened his eyes. "Now, my loved one, how can I assist you today?"

"It's the beach hut. They're tearing it down."

Sam knew Eikia liked the hut. When Sam and Chanel weren't bonking, Eikia did his religious writings there.

Eikia shook his head. "Why?"

"Planning permission."

"Ah." Eikia leant his head back and breathed deep—keeping his eyes on Sam. "Perhaps you are preparing to use physical force?"

Sam shrugged. "Hadn't thought of it. What do you recommend?"

"Well, physical force is to be abhorred—except in the most important of circumstances." Eikia breathed in deeply, kind of an inward sigh. "I believe in the case of the beach hut it may be merited."

"What should I do?" Sam repressed an urge to check his watch. He hadn't flown this guy out from Nigeria, and paid his keep ever since, to get vague little pieces of wisdom.

If he'd wanted that, he would've gone for one of those Indian blokes.

Eikia leant closer. "Who sits at the root of the problem?"

Sam understood the implication of making someone a culprit. If he gave up his wife, the full force of Eikia's power would fall on her. Perhaps Eikia would cast a curse on her, making her breasts and vagina shrivel up, or something else equally horrifying.

Although Sam had never seen one of those curses in action himself, he'd heard stories.

He gave it another moment's thought before saying, "It's my wife."

"Ah." Eikia tilted his head and jerked forward, eyes bulging, as if something troubled his stomach. When he spoke again, he unleashed a full-out shriek. "We must act at once! Bring me a lock of her hair!"

"Er." Sam scratched the back of his neck. "I don't think I have any."

"You must get me some." Eikia crossed his arms. "This is the only way you can help your situation. Come back to me when you have the hair."

Sam nodded and got up from his cushion.

That was all he would get from Eikia—no point arguing. He remembered when he'd pushed him over the problem with the builders who'd come to fix the roof. The next day, Sam had woken up with spots—only a couple, but enough to make him tread cautiously.

Opening the door, Sam watched Chanel approach him at full-speed. He winced, expecting a collision. However, when he opened his eyes, she stood inches from his face. She pecked him on the cheek. "Wha' did Eikia say?"

"Got to get a lock of her hair."

"Well, dere is none of her hair in dis house." She folded her arms and pouted.

"I know, baby, I know. But I've got to find something or they're tearing down the beach hut."

"If you let them tear down the beach hut, I am leave."

His heart raced. "Why?" He narrowed his eyes. "Whatever for?"

"You are such a weak. You need to take control in your life." Her eyes pricked up. "Like you did on the stage."

He clenched his teeth and nodded. "I'll do everything I can." This was all he needed. Probably impossible to find another one like Chanel—not one as packed with life and adventure, no doubt he'd miss her if she went.

She patted him on the chest. Slowly, her hand wandered south stopping when it reached the bulge of his cock in his jeans. She paused, waiting for it to harden then laughed. "You such a big boy!"

Then she skated off, leaving him standing in the corridor.

～

With the fresh ocean breeze blowing through his remaining hair, Sam paced the decking—punching his fist into the palm of the other hand. He was no good at improvising. He remembered the days in the band when the other members had tried to vary sets— usually prompted by the drink or drugs they'd taken against his orders.

Was he the only artist who never played a show *without* a set list?

The only professional in a sea of amateurs?

On the beach, a man and his dog played in the wash. The man threw the stick into the sea and the dog splashed into the waves to fetch it.

Sam's beach hut stood about a hundred yards back. Like a wandering eye, its panoramic window looked out over the bay. He couldn't believe how fast this thing had taken off. He hadn't heard anyone complain about it until he'd got the call today. The whole point was to shield the general public from his and Chanel's sexual antics—so they didn't have to do it, right there, on the sands.

Ridiculous that money could no longer buy privacy on public property.

How much tax did he pay? Probably double the entire village.

Unlike other musicians, who hoarded their savings in offshore accounts or charities, he paid his money to the state and asked for nothing in return—nothing except a little slice of public space where he could relieve his young buzzes with a foxy French teenager.

Why couldn't they cut him a slice?

He kicked a nearby rock, sending it flying down to the beach.

Perhaps he should write to his local MP. He imagined the headlines—Washed up Rock Star Wants Fuck Shack on Public Causeway.

Nothing like kicking someone when he was down.

Wankers.

Up the road, a sand cloud formed as the wrecking truck rolled toward him.

Sam dived into his four-by-four and turned the key. He always kept the key in the ignition for last-minute getaways—the dreaded wife turning up unannounced and pounding seven layers of shit out of anything within range.

He hoped she'd never possess the mental calm to wreck shit into the cars first.

Flicking the car into four-by-four mode, he took to the dunes. He paid no attention to the rocks smashing the chassis—the local garage could take care of that later.

This was a time for action.

The car sent up the loose sand all round him. Eventually the wheels found the firmer sand and Sam made headway to his beach hut. More than wood and glass, the beach hut represented his last bastion.

When he came within ten feet of the hut, Sam jerked back the handbrake. The car swung out in a hairpin. He pulled the keys from the ignition and stepped out into the bright overcast day.

The man and his dog looked at him.

The dog pricked his ears to attention while the man scratched his arse.

It reminded Sam of the stage. That familiar feeling. People looked to him to pull entertainment from the air. The person's circumstance didn't matter. Whether they lived in rural Wales or inner-city London, people craved drama to light up their dim little lives.

Sam leant against the bonnet and waited.

The wrecking truck rolled on. No reinforcements or escort. No accompanying council official in an ill-fitting suit wearing one of those lame skinny ties, driving a Renault Clio alongside.

Sam's pulse beat out an even sixty-five a minute, steady as the wrecking ball that rocked back-and-forth on the back of the truck.

Fifty yards from where he stood, the wrecking truck turned outwards in a neat loop.

Sam realised just what the driver was trying to do—the tricky bastard.

He jumped back into his four-by-four and spun the wheels into action. The wrecking truck increased its speed—trying to disrupt his four-by-four's trajectory. However, Sam was too fast. The vehicles' paths converged and they finished with his four-by-four blocking the truck.

The truck's engine rattled off and the driver stepped down from the cab.

Sam slipped out of his seatbelt.

On his way out, Sam watched the man and dog head back along the shore. He pitied those small town types, no balls to see it through to the end—to risk passing from voyeur to player.

The truck driver was bald with an expansive gut. He wore a loose grey t-shirt and a pair of jeans, decimated at the knee. "Sir? Can't get past your car."

"Yeah? And what're you going to do about it?"

"Please, sir, just doin' my job."

"That's my property you're destroying!"

The truck driver scratched his head then looked around. He creased his forehead and narrowed one eye. "Hey, you that rock star?"

Sam was sure they'd drawn straws to see who got to tear down *rock star* Sam Gax's beach house, so he was certain that this was an act. "I am, yes."

"Yeah, yeah." The truck driver nodded. "You had that Christmas number one a couple of years ago, right?"

Sam grimaced. "That's right."

The truck driver squinted. "Yeah, 'I'm Gonna Stuff Your Stocking'?"

"Yeah, that's the one."

The truck driver laughed. "Won't be playing that one to my grandkids, that's for sure! What a load of rubbish!"

Sam bit his tongue. He wanted to tell him about the million pounds that song had earned him, the golden record on his wall—sprinkled with fake snow.

But this *simple* man wouldn't understand that.

The driver sighed, as if pulling the curtains on memory lane. "Ah, well. Better get on with the job."

Sam stood firm. "Can't let you, sorry."

"Come on, mate. Let's not make things complicated. You're breaking the law and the council has every right to take action."

Sam shook his head. He had a tingle in his stomach, the feeling he got before an arena show, or a physical attack.

It always made him want to shit.

The driver's shoulders dropped and he frowned. "I'm going to have to call the office and they'll tell me to ring the police, is that what you want?"

"What I want is for you to get in that truck, turn it around and go back to masturbating over your Sunday Sport on the hard shoulder."

"Oi!" The driver's forehead wrinkled and his face turned puce. He held his index finger to Sam's nose and wiggled it. "Been to university, you know?"

Sam pushed back the rush of adrenalin. He didn't fancy himself in a fight with a truck driver. "Look, can we make a deal?"

"No way, mate." The driver crossed his arms and shut his eyes, like a stubborn toddler.

Sam looked around him, to the beach hut. What was he going to do to save it? What could he say to this man? He could tell him the truth—he wanted to screw his teenage piece. But he knew that wouldn't work with this man, he probably only got women of Chanel's standard in strip clubs.

Sam sighed. "Can I pay you for your trouble?"

"How much?"

"Five grand?"

The truck driver pouted. "Okay."

Sam grasped the driver's hand and shook it firmly, his eye never leaving the driver's.

The driver sidled up close to him. His breath smelt of curry and breath mint. "All right, show me the money."

"This way." Sam led the driver to his four-by-four. He clicked open the lock with his silver zapper and the truck driver got in the passenger side.

They shot up the sand slope to the beachfront mansion.

Pulling up into the drive, Sam saw Chanel straddling the balcony of the house—topless. A twinge ran through Sam. Obviously, this was her way of cheering him up after his gallant show-down with the council's wrecking ball.

How could she have known he hadn't resolved it down there on the beach?

The driver stared, but didn't say anything. Sam worried about the stories that would come out later. He didn't want to come across as an old sleaze in the press—the typical aging rocker.

Sam got out of the four-by-four as fast as possible and, while the truck driver struggled to undo the clasp of his seatbelt, he shouted at Chanel, "Inside! Quick!"

However, Chanel wheeled herself closer to the edge of the balcony—into the direct eye-line of the truck driver. "Wha'?"

"We have company." He indicated the other side of the four-by-four.

Chanel smiled and made no attempt to retreat.

Sam sighed. There was nothing he could say or do to make her put clothes on now.

Damn neo-feminists . . .

The truck driver got out of his side of the car and Sam showed him up the stairs. When they reached the top, the driver looked Chanel up and down and gave her a shred of a smile. Sam imagined the driver putting that image away to the back of his brain for sordid use later on.

Sam smirked. "This is Chanel, my girlfriend."

"Nice to meet you," the truck driver said.

"*Enchanté.*" Chanel's smile reached back to her ears.

Sam winced, wanting to divert the driver's attention. "Do you like coffee?"

"Yeah, it's all right."

"Well then, I'll make us a cup." Sam waved the truck driver inside.

With a final glance at Chanel, the driver went in.

Once the driver was out of earshot, Sam turned to Chanel. "Would you like to put a top on, sweetheart?"

Chanel pouted and skated off.

Inside, the driver took in the Iron Frazzle wall of fame. He'd look to one disk, squint to read the title then move on, apparently unimpressed.

Sam cast his eyes along the wall. "Heard many of my records?"

"A couple." The driver snorted, the phlegm gathering at the back of his throat—waiting for a good gob. "What happened to your wife?"

Sam squirmed. "Oh, we split up." He chuckled. "Lots of problems, really."

"And that's why the band broke up, is it?"

Sam nodded, trying to look disappointed.

"Shame," the driver said, without emotion. He moved on, approaching the end of the corridor. "So what about this money?"

"Oh yes." Sam laughed. "Almost forgot."

The driver remained stern.

Sam kept his cash at the back of his wardrobe, under a floor tile and inside a combination safe.

The truck driver sat down on Sam's bed to wait. Sam didn't have qualms about the driver seeing where he kept his cash—he only had about ten grand in the house, the rest was in banks or property.

Sam pushed the piles of shoes to one side to get to the safe. Good old, zero-three-six-two. The door clicked and he pulled it open. He dipped his hand in and withdrew ten bunches of five-hundred. He crossed the room and placed the bundles into the driver's waiting hands.

A smug smile on his face, the truck driver brushed his hand across the edges—not bothering to check any of the notes. He got to his feet. "I'll be off then."

"Right so."

Sam led him through the house, into the kitchen. A buzz passed through him. How could he seal the deal? Come across as a nice guy to this truck driver? One of the people? Then he remembered he'd offered the man coffee, but never followed up. He indicated the coffee maker. "Would you like a cup?"

The driver shrugged then perched at the table.

Sam filled the coffee maker with water and ground beans. "So, how long have you been living here?"

"Don't. Live out in Cardiff, dun I?"

He hazarded a glance back at the driver. He seemed happy on his barstool with his money. He turned round, resting his hands on the counter, and drummed his fingers. "Almost ready. Want some biscuits?"

"All right."

"Back in a sec," Sam said, slipping out to the parlour.

On re-entering, he noticed the water boiling inside the coffee maker. He dashed across and pulled off the lid. A plume of steam to escaped as he removed the hot jug. He poured out two cups. "Do you take mil—?"

Sam's eyes tried to interpret the scene playing out in front of him. Topless—still in her roller skates—Chanel stood over the driver.

The driver had his head buried in her breasts.

As Chanel rocked back in pleasure, all Sam's eyes would let him see was the sea view, spread out behind them. "Chanel?"

Chanel groaned.

Sam stepped closer, like someone inspecting a sculpture in an art gallery. He stopped when he was a foot or so from them. The pressure grew in his groin.

His erection rose.

Chanel's hand drew open his fly and—before Sam knew what was happening—he was indulging in the same act that had ruined his marriage.

In their corresponding blue and pink dressing gowns, Sam and Chanel waved off the smiling driver at the door. He padded down the dunes to his truck, walking with a slight limp.

Sam smiled weakly. "Dear?"

"Yes." Chanel kept her eyes on the driver, continuing to wave.

The truck driver turned back every five seconds—perhaps wanting confirmation it hadn't been a dream.

"Are you okay?" Sam said.

Chanel turned to him, a look of disgust on her face. "But, of course."

"It's just." Sam searched for the words. "Well, I thought we weren't going to do that again. What was the idea?"

Chanel sighed and made to go back inside, but Sam caught her and spun her around.

Her pupils dilated as he grabbed her. She loved him to be dominant. She glanced over Sam's shoulder at the disappearing truck driver. "You were not fixing the s'ing."

"What?"

"That's right, what were you doing? Offering him money. That wasn't what he wanted."

"I don't kn—"

She poked him in his bare chest. "You listen! When you brough' him 'ere I saw the way he looked at me."

"But you were topless!"

She continued, "It was zee only way to save the beach hut."

He shook his head.

"What would have happen if you had jus' given him the money?"

"He wouldn't have come back."

"No." She threw up her arms and muttered something in French. "He never would have come back, but I am sure his other friends from the council would have."

"But, why?"

"Because, what would happen? He would have gone back to the office and tomorrow zey would have sen' somebody else here with a new truck."

"Won't they do that anyway?"

"No! I said in his ear to tell zem zee demolition was done. Zey will send the form for you to sign tomorrow and it will be forgotten."

Sam tried to untangle her argument. He thought he understood. And, although he wasn't completely swung, he decided to drop the matter.

It had been this way back in the band too, his wife doing the thinking for the both of them . . . and he was probably making a big mistake leaving Chanel to do that right now.

But, what the hey, life was too short.

He pulled Chanel towards him, letting the happiness buzz inside his chest. "Let's go down to the hut, shall we?"

Chanel frowned then looked at Sam's groin.

But he led her down the dunes anyway.

THE HAMFISTS

The First Gig

KARLY FELT THE TIPS of her fingers stinging. When she sucked on them, trying to subdue the pain, she tasted a little blood mixed in with the metal. She glanced up about her and took in the greenery of the countryside which surrounded them.

Birds chirped about them, and there was a gentle scent of cow manure on the air, just like there always was in the countryside. Everything had more or less recovered following the onslaught of only a couple of moments ago.

Still sucking on her fingertips, Karly felt the weight of her bass guitar tug down on her. The strap, just like always, was digging into the back of her neck. From all the personal practice she'd been putting in this week, a red welt had popped out of her skin.

She'd seen it in the bathroom mirror.

Karly looked back over their band setup.

It was small—it'd been *designed* to be small—but it did the job.

The three-quarter-sized drum kit which Grant sat behind: only a snare drum, high-hat and bass drum. On his bass drum, Grant had spelled out the name of the band: *The Hamfists* using black electrical tape. And he'd made a pretty good job of it too given both the limited space and the difficulty that manoeuvring the tape surely carried with it.

Then there was Jack, who had his electric guitar and a tiny, battery-powered amplifier clipped to his belt.

It'd been Jack who'd first come up with the idea, but Karly couldn't really stomach giving him the credit that he—probably—deserved. She knew, from all her reading of the history of rock and roll, that most bands ended up having their mythology written out by one of the members.

And it was usually the singer.

Thankfully Jack wasn't the singer—nobody was the singer.

They didn't *have* a singer yet.

And, maybe, they never would have one either.

Karly, too, had one of those tiny, battery-powered amplifiers clipped to her belt, and she listened to it fuzz slightly as the sun came out from behind a cloud. She struck one of her bass strings and listened to it reverberate out of her amplifier.

She looked over to Grant and Jack wondering what was coming up next.

She supposed that, if somebody happened to pass by them in a car, perhaps trundling along on a Sunday afternoon drive, that they most likely wouldn't take note of their instruments yet. No, most likely they'd take note of their costumes. And, in particular, the way in which Grant was dressed in a full-bodied ape suit, and the way that Jack wore a Dracula costume with a mask over his face.

Meanwhile Karly wore a clown suit.

Again, with a mask.

This arrangement had really come down to stage fright, no matter what any of the others wanted to claim about the thing.

They'd decided that, to break away from *normal* groups they (one) weren't *ever* going to play real gigs, not in 'traditional' venues, and that they (two) wouldn't show their faces to their audience. If there even was an audience to begin with.

And, out here, in the middle of the countryside, it seemed the only audience they would have was the cows which mooed from the fields surrounding them.

Jack, who'd hastily appointed himself bandleader—or so it seemed to Karly—nodded to her and Grant, wanting them to prepare for another run through their material.

And when Jack nodded, they started into their first song.

'Sergeant Newborth Blues'

As Karly fumbled her way through the bass lines, she once again wondered just who Sergeant Newborth was and just *why* they were playing his blues. But this was one of Jack's songs and so she knew she needed to take a back seat and allow him to enjoy the moment.

Once Jack had got through with the fifth solo—and all before the first chorus—Karly noticed the police car trundling its way along the cracked tarmac countryside road.

They all kept playing.

Not one of them made a motion that they wished to stop.

The police car rumbled to a stop before them and the driver wound down the window, stared out at them. Karly could see that it was a female officer driving and that she wore sunglasses. Her cap was pulled down tight over her woolly blond hair. She didn't call out to them, and she seemed to just be listening patiently to their song.

When Jack brought it to an end, just after the first—and final chorus—and after his seventh solo, there was silence once more.

Or as close to silence as there could be.

Karly could once more feel the gentle *moos* from the cows, and the stirring of the breeze through the long grasses which sprung up at the sides of the road. The smell of cow manure, too, seemed to grow somewhat more intense. And she caught that metal taste of her bass strings in her mouth again, for some unspecified reason.

Karly turned her attention onto the female police officer, who was still staring out at them. Now that there was silence, the police officer deigned to speak. "Got a busker's licence to play here?"

Though Karly felt like one of them should answer, not one of them was forthcoming with the police officer. And so Karly guessed that it all fell to her. She looked to the police officer, swallowed hard and then—from out behind her clown mask—said, "Uh, do we need one to play around here?"

The police officer nodded her head and then glanced out from beneath her windscreen to the road in front. The police officer's nonplussed attitude seemed to suggest to Karly that she ran into these kinds of *issues* all day long . . . that she often drove past impromptu rock groups out in the countryside, all of them seemingly dressed for a Halloween party.

"I'll give you ten minutes," the police officer said, turning back to them. "When I run past here, though, I expect to see you all packed up and gone. That clear?"

They all mumbled an affirmative reply.

It was strange for Karly, seeing the others in the group with her, how their masks rendered them pretty much expressionless.

As the police officer turned her attention back to driving her car, Karly overheard her mumble something about 'bloody kids these days' under her breath.

Just like that, though, the police officer lurched her car on off away from them.

Karly glanced back over the others, gave a shrug, and then slipped the strap of her bass off over her head. Each of them set about packing up their own instruments into their respective cases, and then, as one, they put all of their things into the back of Grant's beaten-up old hatchback and set off.

Not wanting to bother the police officer or the cows any longer than was completely necessary.

The Second Gig

A COUPLE OF DAYS LATER, as Karly was coming out of a lecture at her university, she spotted Grant and Jack sitting off on the side of the concrete fountain in one of the central plazas. The fountain itself, Karly had previously noted, had some plaque dedicating it to somebody or other. But she really couldn't be bothered to read it. That was the thing with the amount of reading she had to get done on her course, it meant that it made her lazy about reading anything outside of what was totally necessary.

Karly trudged over to where Grant and Jack sat, and then set herself down on the wall beside them. Water splashed about the fountain, and it smelled cool and clear. It gave off a remarkably calming effect given how simple of a construction the fountain was.

Both Grant and Jack were deep in conversation, and they paused only briefly to greet her with a pair of smiles before going back under.

Karly sat on the wall beside them, fiddling with stuff inside of her rucksack, just trying to find something to do while she waited for them to finish up their conversation.

She would've known what they were talking about even if she couldn't overhear them.

They were talking about the band.

About The Hamfists.

Their band.

And, more specifically, they were planning out the next gig.

Karly was a little hungry, as she almost always was, and she couldn't help staring out across the plaza to the car park, where a burger van was doing sterling business, and wonder whether she might have enough spare change for a burger and chips rattling about at the bottom of her rucksack.

She thought about ditching these two for a few moments, to allow them to finish up whatever deeply thought-out discussion they were finishing up having, but she decided against it. All things considered, she'd probably snarfed just about her ration of burgers for this week . . . or maybe for this *month* . . . and she was better off going for something more healthy, like a salad. But weren't there all those news stories saying how those boxes of salads you could buy were just as unhealthy as a burger and chips?

Karly's mind remained stuck on that thought when she overheard a pair of chuckles from Jack and Grant, sitting on the wall beside her. And she knew well that they had come up with something. That they had worked out what they were going to do.

"Got a follow-up," Jack said, straight out looking Karly between the eyes.

"Yeah?" Karly said.

They'd only just played their first gig—out in the countryside—so it followed that the next thing that was coming would be their *second* gig.

Karly had to admit that she was somewhat anxious to hear just what the boys had in mind. They *had* started the group as a means to ward off boredom, after all.

Jack glanced back to Grant, and then he nodded to the area before them. "Here," Jack said.

" 'Here' ?" Karly said.

Jack nodded. "The plaza. Seems like the best spot. We'll do it in the dead of night, of course, when there's nobody around.

"Of course," Karly replied, slightly deadpan.

She had to admit that she wasn't *one-hundred-per-cent* down with this whole philosophy that Jack had struck up . . . that he wanted *only* to put on truly guerrilla gigs, the types of gigs that would be nigh-on impossible for the average music fan to track down.

And playing in the middle of the night, in the central plaza of the university, certainly ticked that particular box.

Another of the little quirks of The Hamfists was that Jack had demanded, right from the start, that they never practise. That they simply show up, play through a whole bunch of songs which'd been loosely chatted about on the way to the show, and then get out again.

Their gigs, they'd all agreed—though, again, Jack had been the one who'd been the driving force—would never last longer than twenty, thirty minutes *tops*.

Their first gig had only actually lasted fifteen minutes, but that one had—somewhat rock-and-roll-like—been broken up by the police.

They weren't out to knowingly break laws.

But they were knowingly out to be *obscure*, that much was clear to Karly.

Jack turned to Karly once more, this time grinning from ear to ear. "So," Jack said. "You in?"

What Karly hadn't bargained for, when she'd first heard the idea of playing the show in the middle of the night at the central plaza of the university, was the cold.

The spine-shuddering, skin-pimple-forming, heart-stopping *cold*.

And, as Karly strode her away across the grasses, damp with dew, her bass guitar hanging off her back and her amplifier all ready for action clipped onto her belt, she considered that her clown costume hadn't been designed with the cold in mind.

Perhaps she should've put on a fleece beneath her costume.

But it was too late for that now.

She didn't have time to backtrack.

They'd scheduled to start the show at two a.m. on the dot and though Karly had set her alarm clock for one thirty, she had overslept for a good fifteen, twenty minutes.

As Karly ventured on her way down to the university plaza, she remarked that everything was totally quiet that night. There was simply nothing at all taking place. No sort of an event at the university union. And she guessed that this was all very much part of Jack's plan. He had picked the one night when he could be certain that nothing at all would be going on at the university union.

To ensure that they would be alone.

And that their gig wouldn't be witnessed.

Just as they wanted it.

Jack and Grant were already there, and they'd set up their gear ahead of time. Karly couldn't help thinking to herself that Grant must've had a bit of a tough time in lugging his drums all about campus. He did have a few well-padded cases, of course, but he still needed to cart about his bass drum, his snare and his high-hat.

If the drum kit had been any larger then Karly was certain that he would've needed some help, or have needed to lug his gear about in two loads.

And he had had to cart his stuff about in that ape suit of his *too*.

Maybe it was because it was late at night and nobody much had the energy for full-on conversation, but, without much more than a mumbled greeting, they all took up their places, facing into one another, and they struck up their instruments.

The sound was loud.

Much louder than Karly had expected.

It echoed about the silent university buildings and boomeranged right back at her.

She separated the buzz of her bass from the drums and the guitar.

It sent the hair rising at the back of her neck.

This time they were going to play one of her songs.

Karly smoothed her fingers along the fret board, listening to the bass note getting higher and higher till she couldn't get it any further. Then she played *that* note for a full minute before breaking out into a riff that'd been on her mind for the past week.

Grant and Jack loosely kept up with her as she played.

Karly could feel herself becoming free, almost sensing the music flowing right out from her fingertips, her mind no longer a barrier to her creation. She wanted to speak some words and, there being no microphone, she uttered them to herself, under her breath.

Nobody would hear them.

When the song ended, it felt almost too soon, but Karly knew the rules.

No songs longer than two minutes.

Another of Jack's founding principles.

As Karly stood there, the last note of the improvised song still echoing back off the buildings, she felt a kind of warmth at the base of her gut, and she couldn't help thinking that this—*this*—was just what she was meant to be doing at this specific moment of her life.

That she felt free.

And expressive.

It was around then, as they were all preparing to soar right into the next song—this time it would be Grant's—that Karly heard the voices off in the distance.

Feeling instinctively that the others were about to strike on with the song, she held up her hand for them to pause for a moment. She glanced back at Jack and Grant and, in the moonlight, she saw that they were listening to just what she heard.

She looked about for what they were supposed to do.

Grant wore an expression as blank as the one which Karly was certain she wore herself.

In the end it was Jack who made the call.

Of *course* he made the call.

He was the band leader.

And his opinion was the one which mattered.

He indicated for them to go on, for them to sweep onwards with Grant's song, and Grant counted it off, knocking his drumsticks together before he started up an elaborate rhythm which Karly had a tough time following.

But she *did* follow it.

And as she peered on out through the latex holes in her clown mask, she caught sight of the bodies which belonged to the approaching voices. About a dozen of them. All boys. She stared at them through her mask, losing her place in the song a couple of times.

The boys were all approaching them.

Karly did her best not to allow the approaching boys to bother her. She tried closing her eyes. That seemed to help. When she'd got through with the song, when Grant had decided that they'd been playing for long enough, he brought it to an end with an elaborate drumroll followed by a huge *crash* of his high-hat.

For several moments there was total silence over the concrete-slabbed plaza.

Karly looked out ahead of them, to the boys who had arrived. They all sat down on the wall opposite them, listening attentively. They were all about the same age as Karly and her bandmates.

In the same year at university, probably.

The boys all clapped vigorously when they realised the song was over, and then, just as quickly as the claps had come, they echoed away into nothing once more.

And silence reigned again.

Karly looked to the other two in her band, knowing that it was now Jack's turn to start up a song. She waited patiently till he counted it off scrubbing his palm across the dampened strings of his guitar. Then they all picked the tune up together, all of them playing along.

Till they'd finished *that* time.

When they had, the crowd about them all clapped again, politely, out of appreciation.

Karly looked over the boys' faces. She saw that there was precisely seven of them now, and that they all looked a little flushed, their eyes bulbous in their sockets. Even in the gloom of the plaza, she could make out the dark bags which clung from their eyeballs.

They were waiting for more.

They *wanted* more.

And so Karly and The Hamfists gave it to them.

More applause.

Another song.

The same again.

And again.

Till it was over.

Till they'd played out the prescribed half an hour.

Their show done for the night, Karly shifted her bass off over her head and swivelled it over her back. She expected the boys to disperse, to return to their rooms for the night, with nothing else out here to draw their attention. But they didn't. They stayed where they were. And Karly could feel their eyes on *her*.

When she couldn't stand the feeling any longer, she glanced back at Jack and Grant, seeing that the two of them were packing away the drum kit inside of its padded cases.

Neither of them so much as looked up.

"When you playing again?"

Karly swivelled about. She found herself staring right back at one of the boys. His friends all bobbled about behind him, speaking among themselves. "Uh," Kate said, glancing back at her bandmates: at Dracula and the ape packing away the drum kit. She turned back to the boy, and saw that he had sort of silvery blond hair. "Don't know," she said, now very aware of the clown suit she wore. "That's not really up to me."

"It's not, huh?" the boy said with a slight smile. "Then who's it up to?"

In that moment Karly knew for certain, if she hadn't already, that she had lost whatever input she might previously have had into the band. She had—somehow—surrendered it to Jack, given it to him. Maybe it had happened from the start, when she'd allowed him to lay down the rules, or perhaps it'd happened later on when she'd allowed Jack to decide the locations of their performances. But she tried to concentrate on answering the question.

"It's up to all of us—when we feel like it," she said.

The boy frowned, then glanced at the other band members. "Not got a website or anything?"

Karly found herself smiling at this, though she knew the boy couldn't see that beneath her clown mask. "No, nothing like that."

The boy shrugged and gave a vague smile. "Guess I'll just have to keep an eye out, then, huh?"

"I guess so," Karly replied.

And then, with a brief glance over the group, the boy shuffled off with his friends, all of them trudging along into the night with a sort of dejected cloud hanging over them.

When Karly turned back to the band—back to Grant and Jack —she saw, immediately, that Jack's features had turned to something approximating thunder.

She knew better than to speak with him when he was in one of *these* moods.

K ARLY WOKE UP the next morning still dressed in her
clown suit. She just hadn't got around to taking it off.
She'd been simply so tired the night before that she had slipped
into her bedroom, set her bass down carefully behind the door,
and then dropped right into bed.

As she stirred now, she noted how daylight was already
flooding in around the periphery of the curtain, and she knew that
it was surely sometime late in the afternoon.

If she'd had any lectures that day, she'd missed them.

When she managed to hoik herself up off her squishy mattress,
and got herself showered and dressed, she thought to check her
mobile.

And there she found a message from Jack.

Last 1.
This afternoon.
J

Karly held herself still. She felt like her skull was squishing
down on her brain, but she tried her best not to allow that thought
to get the upper hand on her. She wasn't a doctor, after all, and so
she really didn't have much in the way of a specialised opinion as
far as skulls beating down on brains went . . . and most likely she
was just being melodramatic.

Karly glanced about the place, and then back to her clown suit
which now hung off her wardrobe, all stretched out on its hanger.
She *knew* that she would've been better off renting the costume
from a shop rather than buying it straight out.

By the time that the clock had ticked over to five o'clock in the evening, Jack still hadn't set either a time or place for what was to be The Hamfists' final concert. But Karly tried not to allow it to worry her. She knew this was how things were. That they'd come into this with no hype—not *wanting* any hype—and they'd go out just the same way.

When Karly did get the message through from Jack, she had to read it several times to ensure that it didn't escape her attention. Finally, she did just what she always did before The Hamfists' previous concerts.

She put on the clown costume, grabbed her bass, and shucked on out of her bedroom.

Jack had picked out a place within the university that Karly had never been to before. Though it wasn't like she really had much of a knowledge of the university to start with.

Karly trod along in her clown costume, collecting the stares and gawping looks as the students and members of staff all caught an eyeful of a clown walking about campus with a bass guitar.

Karly clambered up a long flight of stairs—there must've been more than a hundred of them—and to a closed door which was marked: *Solarium.* She held herself still for a couple of seconds before pushing on in through the door and to where her band-mates waited on the other side.

The sight of the place took her breath away.

As she stepped in over the threshold, her eyes were dazzled by the bright setting sun which glared in through the glass. She could see the whole of the campus all stretched out before her, and she had to make a conscious effort not to say something twee.

So, instead, she said nothing at all.

When she glanced about her, she realised that there were rows of steps—seats—which grew up the wall. And she could see that, already, there were about a dozen or so people all sitting up there.

An audience.

One of The Hamfists' greatest adversaries. But they were here.

Nothing they could do now.

And when she looked to Grant and Jack, she was certain she could see the apprehension sketched on their faces. Surely worried about what these people would think.

But Karly hadn't joined The Hamfists to think.

She'd joined them to *play.*

And so they played.

They played the house down.

Everything that they had cobbled together over the past two shows seemed to knit and work, and blend into a single mass. And when Karly struck the very final note of the show, she felt like it was the last note she would ever play . . . at least on her bass guitar . . . while dressed in a clown costume.

The audience swamped them—swamped The Hamfists—and Karly was unbelievably happy. Because she knew that, now, aside from everything else, it was all over.

DEATH TO REDUCTIONIST CINEMA

1

TRACEY seized hold of the glass stem of her red wine and she wondered, if she were to bring it down with a sharp motion against the edge of the coffee table, whether it might snap in such a way as to make an effective weapon.

She would've liked to say that the thing that swung her away from making said rash action, in the end, was mostly down to the moral implications that murder brought on, but, in reality, it was most likely because she was worried that she might do *herself* some harm in the process.

She always had been a selfish cow.

As she breathed in thick aroma of coffee which clung to the air of the *Tunder Independent Cinema Café*, she had to actively repress the urge to scream.

Long and hard.

Right from the bottom of her lungs.

But, as she had done throughout the rest of the evening, she consoled herself with bringing her glass of wine up to her lips and taking a sip.

It was a touch bitter—a hint of vinegar—she wondered if, maybe, it had been 'corked' . . . but she didn't trust herself, certainly not in *this* company, to make any comment.

Because, if she was wrong, there was a fair-to-strong chance she'd get laughed at.

Laughed at by snobs.

Was there anything worse?

The fortifying effect of the wine losing its edge, Tracey tried to further placate herself by sinking down into the plush, leather armchair. The one with all the melted holes which must've been from people putting out cigarettes before the smoking ban.

Or maybe—just maybe—the armchair had once been an 'outside' chair.

She breathed in deeply, trying not to take down too much of the coffee-infested air, and looked over the rim of her wine glass to Alistair.

Or Alistair the Insufferable as she had soon baptised him in her mind.

Alistair was a type . . . an art-house-cinema type . . . he was the *type* which would—nay, *will*—wear a Tam o'Shanter cap despite not carrying the faintest *hint* of a Scottish accent.

He was the type that *will* have a ginger goatee, and which *will* have a strong stench of halitosis constantly hanging around him like a cartoon swarm of flies.

And he is the type who *will*, under no circumstances, shut the hell up . . . like, *ever*.

Gladly, Tracey wasn't completely alone with Alistair since her 'best friend' Kaylee had come along too. And, as it had happened, Kaylee and Alistair shared what could only be termed a *passion*.

A passion for cinema.

A passion which meant that both sides needed to lean their elbows on the dainty, hastily painted, black table which stood propped between them, and jabber endlessly, and with increasing volume, drink after drink after drink.

To say that Tracey had had enough was like saying that she hadn't thought twice about the impromptu dagger-from-a-wine-glass thing.

Make that thrice.

She reached down and, casually, so as not to draw *undue* attention, flicked off a tiny little, white wad of phlegm from the surface of her cosmic-blue dress which she wore over a pair of well-beaten-in jeans.

Said phlegm had managed to escape the corner of Alistair's mouth during an especially impassioned punchline.

She had been hoping she wouldn't have to get the dress dry-cleaned for a *second* time this week . . . the first time had been an unpleasant incident with some oaf—and a pint of cider—in the pub around the corner from her house.

Tracey studied the talking heads. Batted her attention from Alistair to Kaylee, from Kaylee to Alistair, as if she might find something in this conversation that she could *possibly* relate to. Some titbit which she could sink her nails into.

But, to tell the truth, she really knew next to nothing about cinema.

And, to tell even more truth, she really had no intention of bettering her ground-zero level of knowledge.

She looked about the café, looked for someone—*something*—that might be able to drag her attention away from this insufferable pair just for a couple of moments.

Finding nothing, she brought back the table before them, the dark-green bottle of red wine—still about half-full—which stood precariously balanced, and becoming even *more* precariously balanced every time that Alistair chose to bring his fist down, with a *thump*, on the dainty little table.

Tracey felt a smile twitch onto her lips. And she could hardly keep the evil that was bottled up within her from bursting on out in the form of a gaping, open-throated chuckle.

She only realised that she'd laughed out loud when Alistair and Kaylee turned to stare at her, wide-eyed, as if she'd very much slipped right off her trolley.

It was Kaylee who spoke first. "What's so funny about *Two Thousand Wounded Orphans?*"

Knocked off her evil path for a fraction of a second, Tracey couldn't help letting out a bedraggled, "What?"

Kaylee turned to look at Alistair, her dark red hair, which hung in ringlets, bouncing in a way which made Tracey want to ask her just which conditioner she used.

When Kaylee looked back at Tracey, she had a slight smirk lining her lips. "You weren't paying attention, were you?"

"Paying attention to what?" Tracey said.

"To our conversation—to the conversation we were just having."

Tracey looked from Alistair to Kaylee, then back again. She felt slightly nauseous at this routine now. It seemed like she'd been performing it since the Beginning of Time.

Or maybe just a couple of hours.

She guessed she could be melodramatic when she wanted.

Still with the wicked thought on her mind, Tracey decided to hold off for a couple of moments. To play the fool a while. Do something to entertain herself.

"No," Tracey said, "it's just that I found that particular scene in . . ."

She trailed off hoping that Kaylee would fill her in.

She did.

"*Two Thousand Wounded Orphans.*"

Tracey nodded several times in a way she hoped would make her out to look a little tipsy. "Yeah, that's the one, it was that scene, the one with the . . ."

This time it was Alistair who filled her in.

"Where the leader of the orphans—Geoffrey—raises his head above the ruins of his hometown and has his skull blown to bits by a sniper?"

Again Tracey nodded. "Yes," she said, "that's the one."

"And, pray tell," Alistair said, with a raised eyebrow and a sidelong glance to Kaylee. "What so tickled you about *that* particular scene."

Tracey met the two of them, the two of them staring at her, both with varying degrees of smug expressions all smeared over their faces.

Tracey knew just how to answer this sort of a question, she'd learned well from her English Literature classes back at school.

"The pathos," Tracey said.

2

NEEDLESS TO SAY, the conversation between Alistair and Kaylee ticked onwards, with Tracey very much the passenger throughout.

She poured out the dregs of the wine into her own glass, swilled them a little, holding the glass up to the light for some reason she couldn't quite discern, and then knocked them back.

The thing to do now, obviously, was for her to step aside.

To make some excuse and go catch the bus back home.

She would have the house to herself, with Kaylee 'otherwise occupied', and she could go ahead and run herself a nice hot bath . . . pour herself out a large glass of brandy, and lie there till the wee hours with the warm steam billowing all about her.

Since there was only one bathroom in the house—and, by extension, only one *bath*—Tracey and Kaylee often found themselves drawn into conflict when Tracey wanted to take a long soak, while Kaylee, for several hours, had to restrain any urge to pee she might have had. But with Kaylee out of the picture, Tracey would have all the licence she could wish for to simply *go wild* . . . assuming that Kaylee didn't bring Alistair back to *their* place.

But Tracey was fairly certain she wouldn't.

Alistair was the type who, no doubt, would use his *extensive* collection of DVDs to lure Kaylee into his bedroom, and while, no doubt, dragging on about some facet of some obscure—and long-dead—Eastern-European director he would gently—ever so gently—drag his arm about Kaylee's dainty, and freckly, shoulders.

Then, just like a simple *snap* of the fingers, they would fall about the place in a horny embrace.

Being on fairly intimate terms with Kaylee—what with them being housemates and all—Tracey knew that it had been a while for Kaylee . . . a while since she'd had her way with somebody . . . and she knew how a girl got after such a dry spell, why it was just like the cork being squeezed off a long-pressurised bottle.

Tracey looked to the two of them again. Breathed in deep, forgetting the severe odour of coffee about the place, and that she felt the stench getting into her lungs, prickling inside her chest.

They were blabbing on about something which Alistair termed 'Reductionist Cinema'.

Tracey couldn't even *begin* to wonder what that term might encompass.

And wasn't interested in beginning to wonder, either.

Tracey should just go now.

That was the best she could do.

The *noblest* thing she could do.

But, at the same time, that evil continued to lurk near the surface of her thoughts.

And she *just knew* that there was nothing for it.

She would have to have her release.

If nothing else.

And so, looking to the emptied bottle of wine, to the gently smiling Kaylee and Alistair, Tracey hefted herself up from where she'd sunk into the leather armchair, reached across, and, with a neat flick, knocked off his cap.

It flopped to the floor, landing with a kind of impotent *slap*.

Kaylee and Alistair turned their gaze onto Tracey—Alistair looked far more confused than anything else, to have been divorced from his cap so briskly.

In a flat, deadpan tone, Tracey said, "Death to Reductionist Cinema."

"WHAT DID YOU SAY?" Alistair said, scowling, his cap still lying at his feet.

Tracey realised now why Alistair wore the cap, or at least she saw one of the reasons quite plainly, and that was because, though he couldn't have been much beyond his late twenties, he had a distinct circle of missing hair on the crown of his head.

A patch which his scrubby, brown-black hair no longer covered.

She could see that the patch was varying shades of white and pink, and it had that habit that most bald, male scalps had of having mountains of flaking skin.

Before Tracey thought to answer Alistair, she noticed Kaylee catch a glance of said bald patch, watched the way that her eyes flickered over it, and then away, as if the bald patch itself was a separate entity from Alistair and would take offence if it caught her looking.

Tracey turned her attention back to Alistair. To his slightly cocked head. To the way that he held his fist all bunched up at his waist.

He reminded her of a cross fisherman who'd just had some troublesome kid passing by cutting his net with the knife he'd got for Christmas.

"I said," Tracey repeated, and made sure to spell out the words very clearly, so that she wouldn't be misunderstood, "Death. To. Reductionist. Cinema."

Alistair kept up his stern expression for another couple of seconds, and then, almost like a flimsy plaster façade slowly cracking in the sunlight, he snorted a laugh. Wrinkles which, Tracey was sure, had been invisible before, now became pronounced all over his complexion. "You don't have the faintest clue what Reductionist Cinema is, do you?"

Tracey felt her chest tighten a little. But there was no way in hell she was going to allow her poker face to get away from her. She just kept on smiling sweetly at him.

Then she said it again.

"Death to Reductionist Cinema."

Those words seemed to have a physical effect on Alistair. She watched, as the words left her lips yet another time, how he winced at them. How it seemed like there were invisible flies flying about his face, attempting to get at his eyes.

Now that Tracey thought of it, Alistair reminded her of a cow —a cow in a field which was trying to deal with an especially bad fly problem.

Not a bull.

Not even a bullock.

A *cow*.

Alistair turned to look at Kaylee, that same self-sure, *smug* grin playing out over his mouth. But when he spoke this time, he sounded less assured of what he was saying. "She has no idea what she's talking about." He paused, looked to Tracey, met her eye for a fraction of a second, then continued, to Kaylee, "Does she?"

Tracey felt the stiff seconds-long silence which expanded between them all, and she detected a slight frostiness entering the air. She caught a—very distinct—searing glance off Kaylee and she knew that she was treading all over the line now.

That invisible, unspoken line which existed between housemates.

And that if Tracey went much further over it there would be Serious-and-Lasting Trouble between the two of them.

But Tracey realised, increasingly, that she really couldn't care less.

That *these two* had forced her to sit through their whole encounter . . . well, she hadn't *exactly* been forced, not at gunpoint or anything, but Kaylee had been the one who'd floated the idea of her tagging along—of Tracey *chaperoning* her on this 'date'.

Tracey had thought she was taking part in an act of charity above all else, that she was doing Kaylee some great favour as an ally at her side, looking out for her own best interests . . . committed to breaking Kaylee's sexless streak.

Now, though, Tracey was stepping all over the line.

She could turn back.

Apologise.

Make her excuses.

Head on back to that promised—*solitary*—bath.

Finally, Kaylee answered Alistair. "No," she said to him, "You're right, she doesn't have any idea what she'd talking about."

Alistair seemed a touch buoyed by this. Tracey actually witnessed the way that he puffed his chest out, like he was some pumped-up farmyard roaster. And then, with much more grace than she would've expected from a rounded man of his kind, he bent over himself and swept up his cap from where it lay on the floor.

He plonked it back down on his head—worked briefly to align it in such a way so that it covered his bald patch, and then he fixed Tracey with a glare, across the table.

"So," he said, "if you're such an *adamant* critic of Reductionist Cinema then why don't you enlighten me to your opinion of the late-period *neo-modernists?*"

Tracey watched on as Kaylee brought her hand up, those dainty, freckled fingers of hers, and she brushed Alistair lightly on his upper arm. He held up a hand, apparently in response, though he didn't look back at her, and he fixed his stare back onto Tracey.

"No," he said, "I want to hear her out—if she's really got something to say, some argument that will add to the debate then I'm all ears to hear it."

Tracey observed Kaylee's fingers retreating from Alistair's arm, and she watched her shifting expression, from one of slight concern, to one of *dread*.

Though Tracey wouldn't have said that Kaylee knew her *intimately*—they'd been sharing the house for about a year now—she would certainly say that she had nailed down her observations of all Tracey's most obvious trigger-mechanisms.

One of which was challenges.

She just *loved* challenges.

And that was what Alistair had done now.

He had *challenged* her.

Tracey caught Kaylee retreating even further, almost seeming to visibly sink back into herself, almost like she was a snowman—snow*lady?*—melting on a sunny afternoon.

Or maybe it was more like a balloon in a dusty hall slowly losing air and withering down to a wrinkled nothing.

Tracey had Alistair in her sights now, and she didn't intend to allow him to leave.

At least not without scars.

Without batting an eyelid, and keeping the tone of her voice so level that it almost sounded like a rapid-fire machinegun, she said, "Why do you treat your pseudo intellect like it was a seven-foot penis hanging out of your fly?"

4

THOUGH TRACEY couldn't say for certain, she thought that, right after she'd said that comment, and apparently said it quite loudly, that the whole of the café—previously buzzing with conversation, all bucked about with laughing—bubbled down into silence for a long few moments.

Just like always, whenever Tracey took one of these challenges up, she felt her blood pumping harder, felt the pressure at her temples. And her gut sinking down.

Anticipation.

Wanting to see the next move.

That was what these challenges were all about.

With puckered lips, not *unlike* a cat's rectum, Alistair sat on his stool, whatever intellectual point he was about to raise, which he had no doubt hoped to use to bury Tracey—once and for all—thoroughly forgotten.

When Tracey shifted her focus over to Kaylee, she noticed how she resembled more of a wilted flower. One which had been left on a windowsill for far too long without water. And Tracey wondered if she would simply crumble into a fine dust before her eyes.

Tracey looked to Alistair, and then said, "Are you going to answer the question?"

Alistair remained silent. His eyes bulging in their sockets as if she'd just set her pet boa constrictor on him . . . though she didn't have a pet boa constrictor, she'd often pined for one, and never more than right now.

"Huh?" she said, thinking that she heard some sort of a *squeak* dying behind those puckered lips of his.

Nothing.

Tracey looked about her, caught a couple of people looking but she soon glared them away just as quickly. She drew in a deep breath and then sighed it out. "I just don't see why people"—she nodded at Alistair, sort of trying to indicate his whole getup, and no one thing in general—"people like you feel like, just because they're prematurely balding, or because they feel allergic to sunlight, that they have to take their brain, like it was a great big mallet, and strike just about every last person in sight with it."

She paused for a second, allowed her pulse to race a little and then continued, "I mean, does it make you feel good about yourself, that you know something that the rest of us *don't?* What would actually happen if you ever did come up against somebody who knew a great deal about neo-modernist Reductionist Cinema, huh?"

No response.

Just a little hand-wringing, and the aversion of gaze.

"Yeah," Tracey said, "thought so, I bet that if anybody at all *really* took you to task on Reductionist Cinema they'd soon put you in your place, they'd realise that, really, you're nothing else but a whole bunch of hot air."

As Tracey finished up her tirade, she couldn't really bring herself to meet Kaylee's eye, she sort of dreaded it, actually. Though she felt a little bad about having taken this Alistair guy to task, she really hadn't seen any other way.

She had *had* to say something.

And now that she had there *was* no taking it back.

Tracey drew in another deep breath, looked to her emptied wine glass on the table before her, then the bottle of wine, just then realising that she'd drained it only a few moments before. With nothing else for her to do, she got on up to her feet, rolled her shoulders to get out whatever tension she was feeling there, and she walked away from the table.

Away from Alistair.

Who continued to stare down at his writhing hands as if they'd give him the answer—tell him just how he should react to what Tracey had said to him.

As far as Tracey knew, he was fantasising about strangling her.

Not that she'd give him a chance.

Tracey liked to go running—made a point of being an expert at sprinting away from things when they got a little hectic.

To be a Big Girl in the Big City, you needed skills.

As she headed on down the black-painted steps of the cinema, felt the gentle waft of the air outside carrying up, and breathing new life into her cheeks—a welcome break from that stale, coffee-inflected air of the café—she heard somebody calling her name from over her shoulder.

At first, Tracey was sure that it was some acquaintance, somebody who had been watching her up in the café, just biding their time till she broke away.

Oh, how she *hated* those sorts of acquaintances.

But when she did look back, because that night she was wearing a pair of fairly high heels which would've made a running-escape tricky, if not an impossibility, she saw that it was Kaylee.

And that she was bereft of Tam o'Shanter, and wearer.

Perhaps there was some hope in the human race.

Tracey took her in, tried to analyse her as she stood up on the top step, her body silhouetted against the sallow light of the café behind.

"Yeah?" Tracey said. "You coming to give me a telling-off, to tell me that I need to respect your dates a little better than that?" Before Kaylee could reply, Tracey held up her hand, as if to guard against any attempted response. "Don't worry, that was the last one that I'll go along on . . . you know my number if you need any help, so just give me a call."

And, with that, she shimmied on down the staircase, the sounds of the purring evening traffic growing with every step.

She'd set foot on the tarmac pavement, away from the scruffy carpet which clung to the floorboards of the cinema, when she felt a hand on her shoulder.

When she looked, saw the fingers, she caught sight of those freckles.

Knew that it was Kaylee even before she swivelled around to meet her gaze.

Kaylee's eyes spent an awfully long time exploring Tracey's before her lips uttered a sound, and then she said, "I'm sorry for bringing you along—I should've known that you'd have had a boring time."

Tracey gave a shrug. Looked on out across the roofs of the traffic-jammed cars, and to the bus stop which awaited her. She reached up and felt for Kaylee's hands, brushed them with her own fingertips, and then said, "Good luck with that one, and try not to take too much notice of all that crap I just spewed up there, okay?"

Kaylee held Tracey's gaze for another moment and then she gave a nod of her head.

She retreated up the stairs, back off to finish with her date.

Tracey gave her a flimsy smile, and couldn't help turning her mind to the bathtub which awaited her. Coupled with the empty house, it was a real paradise that was stretched out for her this evening. And, in some ways, it was made all the sweeter by the knowledge that there existed somebody like Alistair, not only in the world, but in the same city she lived in.

And that she was hidden from him.

Forever.

She eyed the bus approaching the stop, and shuffled on out of the doorway of the cinema, zigzagged through the traffic and flagged it down.

It was only when she was sat there, on one of the front seats, gazing out at the grey cityscape passing her by, the cars purring along to wherever, that she allowed herself a gentle smile.

Why, tonight, she had quite enjoyed herself.

She knew that *wickedness* gave her a kick—and that 'kick' was what she lived for.

SPEAKING OF ANGELS

1

NOTHING MUCH happens in graveyards. At least, I've always thought as much.

In fact, that might be putting it mildly, because, from what I've seen throughout my life, from what I've *noticed*, the best way I can think to explain them is a domain where everything just seems to stand still.

Those granite stones standing grey and proud as if they might have a chance of still sticking around a hundred years on . . . that they'll easily outlive the lifetime of the one they commiserate. Just standing about. Maybe nothing is forever, but a gravestone might come close.

As I kicked at the crispy autumn leaves with the toe of my battered, muddied walking boots, I couldn't help but feel a chill pass over my skin.

Though I was wearing a windbreaker over the top of a fleece—not particularly womanlike, but whatever—and a pair of just about the thickest pair of socks that money could buy, I felt that same cold.

It might've been the weather, I might grant that, but I'll also throw into the equation that I was walking on past Bortherhame Graveyard, and that it's often been a place where people have seen ghosts. Or where people *think* they've seen ghosts.

Despite the fact I've always been a rational thinker—I was kicked out of my Sunday school class aged eight for suggesting that Jesus was a zombie—I can't help but get those goose pimples rising up on my skin every time I walk past Bortherhame.

It doesn't happen with other graveyards, which is maybe why I paid the sensation so much attention.

Hands stuffed into the pockets of my jacket, feeling the warm woollen inside layer, I looked out over the six-foot-high stonewall of the graveyard, out across all those jagged gravestones, and the raggedy long grass which grew up in random tufts seemingly anywhere.

First thing I noticed was the gate to the graveyard.

And how the lock had been busted right off it.

Look, it's not like I'm criminally minded or anything, but it was pretty simple to see that the rusted-up padlock which had once held firm the iron gates—with their flaking black paint—was now lying on the ground where its shackle had clearly been neatly snapped . . . most likely with a pair of long-handled bolt cutters.

Guess what?

Another shudder . . . though my rational mind was working overtime to make it clear to my inner child that *ghosts* tend not to us bolt cutters to get about the place—if films and whatever else are to be believed then they simply float on through whatever gets in their way.

And then, right as my rational mind got back in control of the situation, I only found myself getting a little more riled at the thought that whoever had busted open the gate to the graveyard was likely far more dangerous—more of a *threat* to me, in any case —than an imaginary ghosty.

Perhaps I should've trudged onwards, away from the graveyard, away from the quaint little chapel that sat in the middle of the burial grounds, what with its slatted roof which was always the focus of fundraising drives—at least that was the kind of propaganda that tended to drop through my letterbox and onto my Welcome mat.

From the looks of that roof, I could only conclude that said fundraising drives, if they hadn't been in vain, had at least not been as successful as might've been hoped.

There were holes all over—several missing tiles—and I could make out more than one bird nest.

I scaled back, turned my attention onto the circumference of the graveyard one more time. I remembered going out on my afternoon walks, passing by the place, and wondering just *why* a place such as this—a graveyard—needed such a sturdy wall.

It was as if it was to try and keep things *in* as much as to keep them *out*.

But that was another thought.

Maybe that snipped padlock was because someone had been trying to get *out*.

Once more, I plugged my rational circuits back in.

Made to continue on with my walk.

If I was feeling particularly the Good Citizen, then I might leave a voicemail for the village constabulary . . . this being a Sunday, there was nobody about . . .

And yet, I didn't carry on.

I hung back.

As if *transfixed* by the gate, and the busted padlock.

And, before I really knew quite what I was doing, I was wandering on in through the gates and into the graveyard.

Among the gravestones once again.

2

I T WAS one of those autumn afternoons where the clouds all look like balls of cotton that've recently been put to task removing mascara. There was a strong scent of rain in the air, and damp grass too, as if an extended warning that rain *was* falling a little way off, perhaps beyond the horizon, but not in some other stretch of reality.

My mouth had long turned sour after I'd chewed my way through the last of my hard sweets—they had this kind of addictive honey taste to them but that taste also had a real habit of drying out your mouth.

I caught another of those chills, and I gritted my teeth so hard that I pinched a little of the inside my cheek with my molars.

The gentle breeze made that ominous *howling* sound—all bark and no bite, as my father would've said—as it blew on through the gaps of the ageing, tumbled-down chapel which loomed above me.

The graveyard was built on a slope. I remember, back when I was a little girl, thinking about whether—maybe—when dead people got buried here, in the graveyard, that they went beneath the earth and started up their own little community.

Kind of like an ant hill.

That they had tea and crumpets and whatever else dead people enjoyed.

Being an adult, though, I reasoned that it was most likely just the natural lay of the terrain. That nobody had ever seen the sense in levelling out a graveyard.

As I felt the burn at the backs of my calves, as I trudged my way up the broken-up concrete pathway, I heard someone sneeze.

That was when I froze.

I got that horrible sensation that someone was watching me.

Though from where, I had not a clue.

The chapel, I saw when I gazed over at it, was clearly deserted.

The notices had been weathered and almost totally conglomerated into the battered old oak door of the place.

I wondered if, in another decade or so, they would simply become *one* with the wood.

If the chapel was still here at all.

If the *graveyard* was still here at all.

I saw nobody around me.

And I came to the conclusion that, whoever it was who had broken in here, into the graveyard, they had to be over the summit of this hill.

I wouldn't see them till I got over the top.

Did I even really *want* to go over the top?

To set eyes on the trespasser?

I did think about it for a while, and then I decided that, *yes*, I had to go and look now.

I guess all my living in a tiny village has given me something of a wary old housemaid's curiosity of life.

Scared of the Big Bad World maybe one day closing in, what with all its crime, and destruction, and decay . . . *violence*.

So, with that in mind, more than anything else just wanting to prove something to *myself* I kept on going, right over the top of the hill.

Down the other side, sitting on the old, grey wooden bench with an etched inscription long ago washed away by the weather, I saw him.

A man.

Middle-aged.

In a suit.

Not a particularly *likely* trespasser.

3

I HADN'T THOUGHT this through at all, and now I found my rational mind catching up with me, and telling me that I should turn around and go back—return home, fire up the wood stove, have a mug of hot chocolate and *damn* the diet. Perhaps pluck a book out of my long-dead father's shelf, in what had once been his study. Lose myself to other realities till bedtime, or till sleep simply caught up with me, took me there, slumped in the battered, old armchair.

But I was too late.

The man turned his head.

I saw him blink a couple of times.

His eyes were no more than inky pools from where I stood.

My feet felt like they'd become glued to the path, and my heart bounced about my chest, as if it might be having serious thoughts on breaking right out through my ribcage.

I waited. Listened to my breathing, loud in my ears.

I felt a drop of rain fall onto the sleeve of my windbreaker, seep through the material and make contact with my skin beneath.

I tried not to notice the chill.

The man kept his gaze locked on me for a long moment, and then he looked away, back off over the graveyard, back to the gravestones.

That was my chance.

I could *easily* have just backed up, headed back home.

But I didn't.

For some reason, when the soles of my boots saw their way to unsticking themselves, I found myself taking on a brisk pace, moving towards the man.

When I came within ten or so paces, I thought he would turn to look at me again. But, as it turned out, he just kept on staring right into mid-air, apparently undisturbed by my presence.

All of a sudden, I felt a flush of anger pass through me.

Sizzle through my blood.

I found myself saying, "You the one who broke the lock off the gates, then?"

The man kept on staring. Looking away from me, as if searching for another horizon, looking for something that—even if he told me exactly how to look—I knew instinctively I would have no chance at all of seeing.

He mumbled something in reply.

I felt my gut twist a little. Only when I spoke again did I realise that it was anger.

"You think this is the *city?*" I said, adding a snap onto the last word. "You think you can just go about the place breaking in wherever you like?"

The man continued to stare off into mid-air.

I wondered if I'd been too sharp with my tone. It was almost impossible to think that only a couple of minutes ago I'd been pretty apprehensive about so much as setting foot into the grave-yard for fear of coming into contact with the trespasser.

But now that I had, it felt only natural that I should be slighted.

This was, after all, *my* village.

My home.

And if I didn't stand up for it—if I made no effort to *protect* it—then who would?

I studied the side of the man's face. Took in what looked to be five or six days' worth of stubble . . . though I have to admit that I've never been all that good at telling much about a man's appearance.

Then I took in his suit, saw that it was well-made, neat silky material, and yet there were a couple of tears—here and there—

perhaps, for as far as I knew, from other occasions when this man had seen fit to burgle his way into some other cordoned-off domain.

He had dark bags hanging down from his eyes, and his face seemed unnaturally slender which made me wonder about the last time he'd had anything to eat.

Only when I looked down, to his feet, and saw that he was missing a shoe . . . that he wore only a tattered black sock with the toes sticking out . . . did the fury boiling up within me show any sign at all of abating.

Guess I've always been a bit of a fool like that—always having a soft spot for those who, for want of a better term, can be described as being 'in need'.

"Look," I began, but then the man cut me off.

He didn't turn to face me when he spoke, choosing to continue staring off into mid-air. I saw that his hair had once surely been jet-black but now had that silvery grey about it.

I wondered if that was premature, or if I'd seen him as younger before.

"My father," he said, his voice wavering all over the place as if in danger of collapsing at any moment, "he is buried here."

I drew a harsh breath. Took in that crisp, *icy* autumn air, and felt another drop of rain—this time at my neck—as I replied, "So's mine."

4

FOR A LONG WHILE, maybe a minute or more, we stood there.

The two of us.

The man continued to stare into space while I stood my ground, staring at the man's barely socked foot, and seeing that the exposed patch of skin was filthy—slick with mud.

Something at the back of my mind told me to *take care of him*, but my rational brain told me otherwise. That I should speak with him. Try to determine his troubles, and then send him on his way . . . or send myself on mine.

Whatever the case was, I simply couldn't see myself shifting from the spot.

However the man had managed it, he had pinned me right here and now.

I decided to break the silence.

"You come here to visit him then?"

Even as I said it, I found myself wincing at the obviousness of it all . . . because what *else* might he have come here to do?

Perhaps something at the back of my mind was telling me that he might just be lying, looking to throw me off the scent before doing what it was that he'd *really* come here for.

And that was *what* exactly?

I leaned my head back, looked over him and saw the bolt cutters which he had apparently used to break his way into the graveyard.

When I checked over the man again, I was certain that he hadn't heard me at all.

Another one of those crisp autumn breezes blew across the

graveyard and I found myself rubbing my hands together for warmth.

I eyed the spot on the bench beside him and thought it over, wondered about just what I was up to here. If I really was going to stay in this, obviously *dangerous*, stranger's company. But, then again, I did feel that thrill passing through me, that tingling sensation that I knew, as much as I tried, wouldn't allow me to simply ship off home.

Or so it seemed.

Just like I always seem to do when I get nervous in someone's company, I began to speak. "You know, when I was a little girl I used to be afraid walking past this place—walking past the grave-yard here." I drew a deep breath, felt it make my lungs billow as if they were nothing more than a pair of cheap rubber balloons. "Used to think there were ghosts."

The man remained in profile to me—his head still bent over to take in the sweep of the graveyard.

I watched his grey eyes. Almost thought I could catch reflec-tions of gravestones in them. Then I knew that I was only making things up in my mind.

A crazy wandering thought dripped into my brain.

The man had said that his father was buried here—just as mine was—and it made me wonder if we might, somehow, be some form of siblings.

Whether our father was one and the same.

I followed his stare, out across the gravestones.

I felt a lump form in my throat as I mentally replayed my father's funeral, saw those charcoal tones of everyone's suits, and dresses, and the shadows which clung to the alcoves of their faces.

I swallowed the lump back then said, my throat drier than I might've expected, "Where's he buried?"

The man remained fixed off in that same *favourite* point in mid-air and then, so slight as to be almost imperceptible to me, he shook his head.

I wondered, for a moment, whether he'd shaken his head at all.

Or if I'd just made up *that* part in my mind.

"You don't know?"

The man continued to face off—over the graveyard—and then he shifted his focus onto me, and I took in his shrivelled face for the first *real* time.

"No," he said, firmly, and, apparently, *finally*.

"Would you like me to help you look?"

For a long moment he remained silent again. I was sure that I heard him sigh slightly, under his breath, and then he said, "Okay."

5

A S WE STEPPED among the gravestones, I couldn't help but
flash a glance, every step or so, to the man's exposed foot,
to the skin which the black sock no longer covered.

I watched as the gunk from the path—the muddied leaves—
stuck to the material of the sock, and to the man's skin. How it had
turned his skin a bright pink shade.

I noticed that he was shaking from his shoulders—shuddering
in a way that I could see he was consciously fighting.

He didn't want me to notice he was shaking, that he was cold.

Together, we reached the edge of the graveyard, the opposite
end to the gate where the man had broken in—and through which
I had followed him.

The simply, stony, and yet—as I'd always thought before—
unnecessarily *high* wall marking the periphery of the graveyard.

Apparently it hadn't been high enough to keep this man out.

Or, at least, the height of the wall was more or less in vain if the
padlock could so easily be clipped from its place and entrance
stolen.

I looked to the man. "These are the freshest graves," I said,
thinking about how my own father's grave was along this row.

Right at the end there.

And that got me thinking about the last time I'd come here, to
visit . . . and how it must've been six—no, *seven?*—months
previously . . .

Again, my rational mind kicked in, reminded me that the
dead inhabited nothing more than the grimy mud beneath our
feet. That there was no other world for them to go to. And that
they would have placed no importance in what the living got up
to once they were gone, because there was nothing to think

about once someone had tripped on over—slipped into the next reality.

Into the abyss.

No, my father wouldn't mind my not visiting him now.

Because all that remained of him in this world was the memories housed in my skull.

And, soon enough, the worms would have at that too.

The tone of the man's voice was so husky, so dry, that I almost missed it. Perhaps I wouldn't have noticed he had spoken at all if he hadn't extended his skeletal finger, pointed off along the row of gravestones. "... There," he said.

We stopped our pacing. I looked along his muck-stained fingernail to the place he indicated—to the gravestone there.

For a second my heart stuck in my chest. I felt it flutter about like a trapped moth frantic to break free, knowing that its life was on the line.

Because I thought he *was* pointing to my father's gravestone.

But, as we trudged closer to the spot, I noticed he wasn't pointing to my father's gravestone, but to the one which stood alongside it.

"Graham Laxley," I said, before even thinking it over.

The man blinked a couple of times. For the first time in our acquaintance, I was sure that I spotted a fresh sheen of light pass across the surface of his eyes. That I saw some sort of feeling there.

I took this as my opportunity to speak. "He was our neighbour," I said.

And then thought to myself about how my father had been the one to spot him. That my father had been pruning the rosebush at the back of the garden when he'd spotted Graham lying on his back—red-faced—blue lips jabbering something or other.

By the time the ambulance arrived, he was dead.

It was funny, in a way, those games that we played—me and my father—how we'd often joke about the village, about how it was turning into a *ghost* town. We'd chat about it constantly. An in-joke. Like our personal sweepstake on who would be next to pop their clogs.

Little did either of us know that it would be my father who would be next to go.

That he would occupy the lot beside Graham Laxley—that they would turn out to be neighbours for the rest of eternity . . . whatever *that* really meant.

I felt that shuddering warmth rising up about the rims of my eyes. Knew that if I kept on thinking things over any longer then I would start bawling myself.

And I'd done enough of that.

Dad was dead and buried.

In the ground.

What little remained of him beneath our feet.

Six feet under.

Not coming back.

Decaying carbon remains.

Those little electric sparks bouncing about his brain that had once been his personality—his sense of humour—whatever had made him *human* . . . that had been extinguished when he'd slipped, and fell, and snapped his neck while reaching up his bookcase, for that elusive book right at the top, the shabby one that he always kept out of the way, the one that he often thought I never knew anything about: the one that held his Great, Big Secret.

The secret which he would've liked to take with him to his grave, but which, in his moment of dying, he passed onto me.

Those letters.

Love letters.

From some woman . . . my *mother?*

Who's to say?

The pages had all been yellowed, all turned up at the corners. The paper obviously well-thumbed, gone through on many a sad day, all those days when my father had—apparently—needed just a little auxiliary love in his life.

I burned them in the garden the day of his funeral.

Just as I'm sure Dad would've wanted.

Though I don't believe in ghosts, angels neither, there is still a great sense of pride in justice done to someone's memory.

Even if that memory is only inside your own head.

We stood at Graham Laxley's gravestone. The two of us. We could almost have been man and wife, perhaps brought here together by some unseen force. Anyone sneaking a peak over the wall of the graveyard might've believed us *both* in mourning.

But, speaking for myself, I knew that I wasn't.

And I caught the feeling that this man, though he had made a pilgrimage, of sorts, wasn't in mourning here either. No, in fact I was almost certain that he had come here in search of much deeper, more compelling answers than something so simple as closure.

We stood for a long few moments before the man spoke again.

"What . . . what was he like?" he said, his voice still husky, weathered either by drink or lack of sleep . . . or perhaps both.

"Graham?" I said, as if mulling this over. "He was our neighbour—lived right next door."

I thought hard for something—*anything*—that I might impart to this man. But how much do you ever *really* know about neighbours, beyond small talk and unfounded gossip?

Still, I did my best.

"He, uh, he enjoyed tending to his garden," I said finally, at the same time thinking that the same could be said for just about anyone in the village—any of the retired and alone.

The man continued to stare down at the gravestone, his eyes

glazed over now as if I was parting the mists for him, and drawing some kind of compelling portrait of the man—the *father*—who, apparently, he had never known.

"And," I continued, "he would often invite us round for tea . . . in his conservatory."

As I spoke those words, I thought about how me and my father would joke about those occasions. How, as my father would close the door on his next door neighbour, he would mime hanging himself with a thick piece of invisible rope.

My father almost always found some excuse—some way of getting out of those meetings with Graham Laxley.

That became a game too.

He would think of something more and more creative each time: a leaking roof tile in *urgent* need of attention, a case of termites in the attic, a dead goldfish so dear to him that it rendered him unable to function on any emotional level beyond babbling incomprehension.

Graham Laxley never asked after the excuses.

He never made any comment to suggest my father was attempting to avoid him—pushing away the extended hand of companionship.

I blinked a few times. Felt the billowing mist moving in.

It was getting on, into the late afternoon, and I knew that, soon enough, a chilling fog would roll in to smother the whole of the graveyard, and the village too.

That was, as I'd often thought as a little girl, when the ghosts would *really* come out to play.

As the man continued to stare at the gravestone, I said, "Do you have somewhere to go?"

The man flinched.

It was odd, I was struck by a note of recognition in the man's face: something which seemed to remind me of Graham Laxley.

Something I couldn't quite put my finger on.

The man batted his eyelids several times, as if clearing away unseen mists.

Or maybe he had begun to cry without my noticing.

Then he said, half turned towards me, ". . . Train station?"

"The train station?"

He nodded, thickly.

So that was how he'd got here—it made sense, I supposed.

I couldn't quite imagine he had *driven* here in the state he was in . . . not without leaving his car wrapped around a tree, or lamp-post, or worse . . .

I gave him a sliver of a smile. "Come on," I said. "This way."

6

I DIDN'T QUESTION HIM when we passed by the bench he had been sitting at and he bent down to retrieve the bolt cutters.

Maybe I should've been thinking more clearly.

Have believed it might be a threat.

But, for some reason, I felt infinitely calm with this man—supremely *un*threatened by him.

I walked with him along the narrow, single-lane cement road—all dotted with potholes about the edges, all those places that time had long forgotten.

I gave the man instructions on how to reach the train station.

It wasn't difficult.

Simply a matter of following the road, through the fog which was rolling in, for about ten minutes . . . but surely if he had arrived by train to the village some level of instinct would kick in eventually.

Or perhaps he was further gone than I'd imagined.

When the man turned into me, I thought we might end up embracing.

But, as it turned out, he handed me the bolt cutters, mumbled something about the house opposite us, that he had liberated them from a garden shed around back, and, apparently, was leaving them in my possession so that I might be the one to return them.

Then again, I supposed that, in his condition, it only made sense for me to be the one to try and explain.

After all, many of the elderly in the village would not bat an eyelid at calling in the police for the matter.

Many of them were fiercely defensive of their independence, and their capacity to ward off the great evils of this world.

As I watched the man plod his way along the road, the leg of his suit trousers brushing against the overgrown grassy bank, I observed the mist tumbling over him. Concealing him. Making him disappear like a cheap magic trick. And, moments later, nothing of him remained at all.

I returned the bolt cutters to the appropriate house, but not without first returning home to write a note which—I hoped— might explain all.

It was only once I'd got myself back home for the second time, back into what had once been my father's favourite armchair, a mug of hot chocolate nestled between my hands, that I thought of the man, wondered if he would be okay, if he would get wherever he needed to go.

I tried to rid myself of that nagging feeling of neglect—to tell myself that his troubles were none of mine—but I couldn't help bucking up onto my feet, and heading out of my home once more.

Heading to the train station. A simple, deserted platform. Half lost in the fog and the arriving night. No sign of the man.

I wondered if he'd even managed to arrive at all . . . or if he had collapsed into a ditch along the way, perhaps twisted an ankle.

I retraced my footsteps, back along the country road, headed back into the village, but I found no trace of him, even with the assistance of the electric torch I shone all about the foliage.

He had gone . . . whatever *that* meant.

When I returned home, my mug of hot chocolate was cold in that way which makes my toes curl, my skin squeeze into pimples, so I decided to tip it out into the sink.

As I headed back to my father's study, back to the open fire and to the bookcase stuffed to bursting, I couldn't help but stop off and look out through the windows.

Into the back garden.

To my father's rosebush.

To the one he had spent many an afternoon pruning.

. . . And thinking about *what* exactly?

Even as I stood there, staring out across the lawn, and the fog which smothered it, I knew that I would never find out, but what did it really matter?

If I didn't know my father's *every* last secret.

He had brought me here, after all.

To my home here.

In the village.

And, right away, right *then*, I knew also that it would be the place *I* would die.

Someday they would bury me in that graveyard and maybe— just *maybe*—other visitors would stride about my grave and talk of my name with little recollections, and empty memories. Because those would belong to them.

And no one else.

Least of all me.

FIVE SUITS & A COFFEE CUP

T HE SUN STREAMED DOWN through the elm trees. It was autumn. Just the beginning, actually. The leaves had got that whole crispy aspect to them, and they'd only just begun to stir from their branches, and to break off under their own weight.

To drift down to the earth.

Oliver Ghorthnaught laid his briefcase down at his feet, and took his seat on the white-washed metal chair in the concrete-slabbed courtyard. He was the first to arrive. Just like always.

He made a point of it.

It was good to get to places early. It meant that he could do just what he was doing now.

It meant he could reach inside his suit-jacket pocket and fish about for the foldout mirror he kept concealed within.

It meant that he could give himself that all-important once-over.

Which he did now.

Fine.

Just fine.

Pinched eyebrows. Pert, proud, well-blooded lips.

And a crisp, clean, and chiselled, silver-grey suit.

A fine specimen of a man.

That was what they all said about him.

Behind his back.

He was certain of it.

With a final flick through his smooth, well-gelled blond hair with a comb he produced with the efficiency of a flick knife from his suit pocket, he sat himself back, arm resting casually on the back of his chair, and he waited.

Waited for them to come.

Just like clockwork, they arrived.

Their own suits.

Their own briefcases.

Each of them took their seats until each one of the metal chairs drawn up at the small table was occupied.

In the end, it was Oliver himself who noticed the coffee cup which stood in the centre of the table. There was something . . . something *unseemly* about the sight, and he made a point of looking to the others, looking for their reaction.

But they could only stare.

Like a whole bunch of stunned *sheep*.

Sometimes Oliver believed that he was the only one among them with so much as an original thought in his body. He reached out for the cup—one of those disposable, cardboard contraptions with the extra cardboard strip wrapped about the base so as to prevent burnings of the hand.

Thoughtful.

Oliver wondered who had thought up that cardboard strip. And how much of a cost that person had added to production. He wondered if it had once been a common complaint—people wanting to grab hold of their hot coffee so badly, with places to be —not to mention people to see—that they simply had no time to *stop* and to *drink*.

Were those people really *human* any longer?

Oliver smiled to himself wryly. He often allowed himself to get carried away like this. He allowed his own thoughts to go all *wild* on him, and for his mind to begin to wander. He blamed it on lack of stimulation. His job gave him none of that. All it gave him, in retrospect, was simply a lot of time alone.

To be inside his own head.

Oliver's fingertips were about a hair's breadth away from the cup when he snatched his hand back. When he left the coffee cup there on the table.

It was better this way.

"What do you think it means?"

None of them knew each other, or referred to one another, by name. Oliver, though, had already developed ways of describing the others to himself within his own head.

The one who had just spoken Oliver knew as the Redhead . . . because he had flaming-red hair sprouting from his scalp.

"Nothing, probably nothing."

That was Dormouse.

Called that name for obvious reasons . . . i.e. He looked like a *Dormouse*.

"Should we break and meet again tomorrow?"

This time it was Golden Nostrils, so named for the downy, blond hair which protruded from the pair of his nostrils.

"Suspicious, no doubt about it."

That was Blackheads.

The one who seemed to always have a whole bunch of black-headed spots clogging up the pores on his cheeks.

Just like always, Oliver ensured that he was the last to get his own word in, and he said, "Let's just get on with what we came here to do. Forget the cup's even there."

The others didn't seem too convinced to begin with, and Oliver noticed how Redhead, in particular, was extremely reluctant to look away from the impromptu centrepiece.

He finally did, though.

And Oliver felt the attention of the group all centre onto himself.

This was how he liked it.

The perfect way for it to happen.

When Oliver had convinced himself that they all had eyes for him, and that the coffee cup had slipped from the group concentration, he shifted his attention to the briefcase he'd brought along, and which he'd left at his feet.

He brought it up into his lap.

Their eyes followed him all the way.

It was an unusual briefcase, in some respects.

Perhaps the greatest respect of all was that it was made from calf hide.

Only the finest, the silkiest he could find.

Some of the others in the group, Oliver could tell, saw this choice of briefcase as a touch self-indulgent, but Oliver knew that only the finest was for him.

The others could stick to their dour leather—black and brown —cases if they wished.

But don't let them ever try to challenge him for his position as leader of this group.

Oliver snapped the pair of clasps free, and he brought the well-oiled hinges of his briefcase open. He set the briefcase down onto the table, first before him, and then he swivelled it around so that the others might see.

As Oliver observed them staring into his case, he thought that they all resembled a group of explorers from one of those ghastly gold-rush films from the forties and fifties. That crutch scene where everybody needed to peer down into some hole at some unseen treasure.

Oliver smiled to himself and waited the few beats it would take for them to fully absorb what was positioned before them.

Redhead was the first to speak: "Is that . . . ?"

Blackheads: "It can't be . . ."

Golden Nostrils: "No, I don't think . . ."

Dormouse: "Never before, had I . . ."

Oliver smiled more widely. He reached out and flapped the

case shut with a hearty *smack*, and laid it back down on his lap. He rested his elbows on the top, and looked to the others, wondering what they would say to him.

But, when nobody spoke, he supposed he was going to have to push them into action.

"So," Oliver said, "Any takers?"

Their faces remained like gaping voids, clearly unable to express even the most basic of their desires. Oliver wondered if he should help them out a little more.

"I thought we could start the bidding at a million?"

Blank expressions.

All those poor—*poor*—poker faces.

Really believing that they could resist showing how much they really *wanted* what Oliver was offering.

Oliver glanced to the coffee cup in the centre of the table.

It remained where it was.

Dormouse was the first to make any sort of a *squeak*. And it was nothing more than a *slight* squeak—the vaguest of inclinations of his head accompanying it.

Then the rest followed.

Oliver sat back in his chair, glad to see that things had gone so swimmingly here. He had believed that they would find it difficult —if not *impossible*—to resist what he had to offer.

And he had been correct in that assumption.

One by one, the men in suits all got to their feet, taking their briefcases with them.

On their way away from the table, they each paused to shake Oliver's hand.

He gave them all the same firm grip, and made a point of meeting each of them by the eye.

He waited till they'd all left him—Dormouse, as always, being the last one to shift on out of the courtyard. Once the men had left, the sun came out from behind a cloud, and Oliver, for a few seconds, savoured the sensation of warmth on the shoulders of his suit.

Oliver reached over and took hold of the cup. He popped the lid of it and peered inside.

There was nothing there, of course.

He had bought the cup of coffee not ten minutes before the meeting here.

But it had been enough.

Enough to scare them into thinking that somebody might be listening.

That their higher-ups might be listening.

And that they couldn't afford *not* to take what it was Oliver was offering.

For all the men in suits had known, Oliver might've been their boss . . .

With another wry smile, Oliver stepped on over to the bin— encased in plastic—and he deposited the coffee cup inside.

He listened to the gentle *swish* as the cup fell against the plastic bin liner within.

And as he headed on away from the courtyard, he noticed that there was a certain skip in his step.

A skip that hadn't been there before.

AUTHOR'S NOTE

Thank you for taking the time to read one of my books. If you would like to hear about my latest releases you can sign up for my newsletter here: www.tjbainz.com

Thanks for reading!

TJ Bainz

Letters To Another
A Short Story Collection